THE WILCO PROJECT

by

Daniel Springer

Enjoy...

THE WILCO PROJECT

DANIEL SPRINGER

To my wife, Sheri, and my kids, Steven and Madison — I love you all.

There are many people that provided invaluable help, support, and guidance to me during the writing and editing of this book—for those that I have inadvertently left out, I sincerely apologize. Big thanks to Dr. Andy Solomon for seeing potential in a rough story and to my editor, Danielle Thorne, for helping me polish that story into a novel. Thanks also to Mom, Dad, Wanda Johnson, Marty Springer, Teri and Clint Locke, Missi Aspiras, Selma Leach, Steve Frazee, Vincent Salazar, Jeff Valmus, and Lee Ziliak, for providing honest feedback and ideas. And lastly, thanks to my friends and fellow authors from the Florida Writers Association, Eugene Orlando, Kaye Coppersmith, and Paul DuBose.

Prologue

Saturday, November 8 -- 12:07 A.M.

Not much farther. She quickened her pace using the intramural softball field's chain link fence to guide her to the woods directly beyond. The light over the equipment shed fifty feet behind did not reach this far, and the moon was new, little more than a sliver. With the tree line only a few strides away, she stopped, a shiver rippling through her body.

This is totally stupid. She knew an attractive female student should not wander alone in a remote corner of the campus—especially at midnight—but she had fought too hard to give up now. She swiped a forearm, prickly with goose bumps despite the muggy air, at the sweat droplets streaming down her face.

With trembling fingers, she pressed a key on her cell phone and studied its color display. The game screen glowed with a digital map of her immediate vicinity. The white icon positioned to her right on the map, just beyond the outfield fence, made her smile.

Good. No one figured it out and got here before me. This just might give me the power I need to win the game.

There were no red enemy icons on her screen.

Looks like no one is following me.

She rubbed the phone's display with her shirttail. *I hope this damn thing works.*

She held her breath and listened for sounds of other players in the area. Nothing. She exhaled.

Okay, move, girl. A few more feet of chain link and then the woods. That's where it is. You have to go into the woods to get it.

She reached the end of the fence, and a wave of panic overtook her, almost buckling her knees. Adrenaline surged into her bloodstream, her heart rate soaring. She dropped the phone and grabbed the fence post with both hands, holding on hard against the urge to turn and sprint back to the safety of the campus.

She took deep, even breaths and willed herself to calm.

Damn it—get a grip.

She pried herself loose from the fence and flexed her aching fingers.

I guess I already had a pretty good grip.

Somehow, she managed a smile.

Squatting, she picked up the phone and brought it to eye level. Thumbing the button on the keypad again, she scanned the phone display. The map was still clear of enemy players. She wrinkled her nose at the stench of body odor and sniffed her armpit. She reeked.

Is this stupid game worth it?

She stood for a moment debating her question. Estimating she would have to go no more than thirty feet into the woods to grab the prize, she gnawed her lower lip.

Yes, I've come this far, and I'm not turning back now.

She moved a dozen steps into the woods. Darkness forced her to navigate through the trees and sparse underbrush using the backlit display of her cell phone as a makeshift flashlight. She squatted next to the trunk of a large oak tree to rest and get her bearings. Surrounded on all sides by woods, it took a couple of seconds for her eyes to adjust. Twisting oak branches and spiky palmetto fronds, which moments before her panicked mind had identified as horrible monsters, focused into harmless trees and bushes. Her racing pulse eased, and she relaxed her grip on the phone.

This isn't so bad.

She inhaled several deep breaths, the pungent smells of the earth and trees filling her nostrils as she listened to the rhythmic chirping of the crickets. She sponged the sweat from her face with her shirtsleeve and chuckled.

Twenty-one and still afraid of the dark, sheesh.

Studying the electronic map on her phone's display, she determined that her current position placed her almost directly on top of the prize's white icon. She smiled.

Only a few more feet to go, and the prize is mine.

Ready to push on, she stood. Her head whipped around when she heard a noise, like something rustling the fronds of a nearby palmetto bush. Halting, she listened as a fresh batch of adrenaline exploded inside her. Silence. She rewound the tape in her mind and replayed the sound.

Yeah, she nodded, *nothing to worry about, that sound came from deep in the woods.*

Seconds ticked by as she replayed the sound again and again until she convinced herself she didn't know how far away the noise had occurred. She stood frozen for a minute, which seemed like hours, listening for further movements over the thundering sound of her beating heart.

Convinced a fallen branch must have caused the rustling, she keyed the cell phone and studied the map again to verify no other player had somehow managed to sneak up on her. The map still showed no enemy icons.

Damn it—stop acting like a paranoid wimp!

She drew in a deep breath.

This is just a silly game.

She exhaled and took a small step away from the tree, deeper into the woods toward the prize. Just before her foot touched the ground, a twig snapped behind her. Spinning around, she flinched as the vague outline of a human figure rushed toward her.

Paralyzed, she tried to scream, but before the sound left her throat, the lunging figure clasped the back of her neck and clamped a gloved hand across her mouth. Arms flailing, she kicked backwards but failed to connect.

The hand gripping her neck slipped down around her waist, pinning her arms and cinching her body tightly against her assailant. Not able to move or utter a sound, she was as helpless as a moth entangled in a spider's web. The more she struggled or tried to scream, the tighter her captor squeezed her close. After thirty seconds of unsuccessful thrashing and kicking, she fell limp with exhaustion, guttural sobs backing up in her throat. No longer able or willing to fight back, the realization hit her—the game was over and she would probably never leave the woods alive.

Chapter One

Professor Steven Archer gazed out of his second-story office window at the deserted street and sidewalk below. The sleepy college campus had yet to come to life that warm Saturday morning. Beyond the street, in the center of a grassy courtyard, golden beams of sunlight filtered through the branches of an enormous oak tree that would later provide a shady spot for students to congregate and study. The clear blue sky, marred only by the fading remnant of a silvery jet contrail, signaled the beginning of a perfect day—the type of autumn day Floridians earned by surviving the unbearably hot and sticky summer when the temperature and humidity rose to well above the ninety-degree mark.

Longing for soft sand beneath his feet, the rhythmic sound of waves landing on shore, and the salty sea air that accompanied a jog down the beach, he sighed and resumed reviewing the thick stack of paperwork piled on his desk. He reminded himself that life would soon return to normal as his team of student programmers had nearly completed the software development project, one of the most technically challenging efforts he had ever attempted.

He scrawled a note on the project plan, pleased with the software testing to date. The student project team, some of the brightest computer programmers he had ever taught, had somehow managed to remain ahead of schedule and, barring a catastrophe, would finish the project on time. He smiled.

I am so proud of these kids and what they have accomplished. No one in the industry, let alone a bunch of college kids, has ever done a project like this.

Public game testing had been extremely successful and he anticipated the test game conducted the previous night had gone smoothly as well. He looked forward to the debriefing from his project manager at their lunch meeting later that day.

The ring of Steven's desk phone interrupted his peaceful silence. He chuckled—the tranquility had been too good to be true. His eyebrows narrowed. If last night's test game had encountered a major problem, he should have heard about it by now. He picked up the receiver.

"This is Professor Archer."

"Steven, it's Frank."

"How's my favorite detective?" Steven smiled—he had not spoken with Frank in several weeks.

"Not so good, my friend." Frank paused, and then continued in a more somber tone. "A female student's body was found in the woods behind the intramural softball field this morning."

"A student? What happened?"

"We're not sure yet, but we're treating the case as a homicide. That's all I can tell you over the phone." Frank paused again. "Steven, I need you to come to the crime scene right away."

"What? Why do you need me?" Steven dropped his pen, and the color drained from his face. "Oh my God, Jenny. Frank, is this about my niece, Jen—"

"Hold on," Frank interrupted.

Steven swallowed hard, his insides revolted at the thought that this homicide might involve his favorite niece. In less than a second, the detective came back on the line.

"Listen to me, Steven. I know you're concerned about your niece, but I can't talk with you about this over the phone. Something urgent has come up here at the crime scene, and I've got to go. Meet me here as soon as you can, and do not speak to anyone about this."

"Frank, is it Jenny? Is she okay?"

Instead of an answer, Steven heard a click and then dead air.

Steven grabbed his cell phone and bolted out of his office. He dashed down the stairs, taking two at a time and exited the computer center building trying to decide if it would be faster to drive to the crime scene or run.

Leaving his car keys in his pocket, he sprinted across campus toward the intramural softball field. He speed dialed Jenny's dorm room on his cell phone and got no answer. Desperate to reach her, he tried her cell phone, and again, no answer.

Steven's lungs burned, and a stitch gnawed at his side. He pumped his legs harder. Tears flooded his eyes. Jenny must be dead, and Frank had not wanted to tell him over the phone. He must have called him to come to the crime scene to identify Jenny's body.

He slowed to a jog, unable to keep up the fast pace. *This is all my fault.*

After all, he had convinced Jenny to attend his university. He had promised her and her parents he would look after her. How would he tell his brother about his precious daughter? Just an eighteen-year-old freshman in college, Jenny had her whole life ahead of her.

Walking now, Steven wiped his eyes and forced himself to replay the phone conversation with Frank. Frank had never actually said Jenny was dead.

Maybe Jenny's not the victim, he reasoned.

She might not even be involved. There could be other reasons Frank had not revealed details about the body to him over the phone. Nearing the intramural softball field, he began to sprint again.

As Steven approached the woods behind the center field fence, Frank ducked under the crime scene tape and rushed to meet him. When they came together, Steven stared into Frank's eyes, unable to speak as his lungs labored to repay the oxygen debt created by his sprinting. He clutched at his sweat-soaked shirt, while his other hand swatted at the gnats buzzing around his feet and wet sandals, drenched from running across the dewy grass. Still breathing heavily, he could barely speak.

"Is she—" Steven gulped a breath of air, "Jenny...is she dead?"

"Steven, you need to calm down and follow me."

Steven thrust his hands on his hips and shouted, "Frank, damn it—"

"Keep your voice down and follow me," Frank ordered.

Frank led Steven away from the uniformed cops patrolling the perimeter of the crime scene. They walked thirty feet to the thick yellow police tape tied to the outfield fence. The tape looped around the trunks of huge oak trees and then back around to the barrier. They ducked under the tape that formed a rough circle with a diameter of about one hundred feet. A smallish body, covered by a white sheet, lay in the center of the circle.

Towering oak trees blocked out the sunlight leaving the area in shade. Because of the thick ceiling of tree branches, the white sandy ground lay barren except for thin piles of dead leaves and twigs and clumps of knee-high palmettos scattered every few yards.

A few feet inside the yellow tape, they stopped. Still struggling to catch his breath, Steven bent down and placed his hands on his knees. Frank squatted and looked Steven in the eye.

"Steven, I know this might be difficult for you, but —"

"Detective Diaz, get over here, now," said a crime scene investigator who stood over the sheet-covered body about fifty feet away. There's something here you've gotta see."

"Stay here," snapped Frank, pointing to the ground at Steven's feet. Before Steven could protest, Frank dashed toward the beckoning crime scene investigator.

Swearing to himself, Steven stood straight. He lifted his arms over his head, filled his lungs with oxygen and exhaled. Although his breathing had nearly returned to normal, his mind raced out of control.

Oh God, why Jenny?

With a shaking hand, he wiped the sweat from his eyes and scanned the scene, looking for clues, trying to make sense of the situation.

On his tiptoes, Steven looked past the half-a-dozen crime scene investigators in olive-green coveralls working at various places inside the yellow tape. Visually scouring the area, he strained to identify a piece of clothing or a shoe —anything to rule out Jenny as the victim. Nothing. He squinted at a forensic photographer who, at the direction of an older man in a suit, who Steven guessed to be a senior homicide detective, alternately snapped pictures and shot footage with a high-end video camera. Nothing.

He had purposely avoided looking at the white sheet, but now he forced himself to turn and stare toward

Frank and the CSI, huddled over the body. A wave of panic hit him, and he fought off the urge to retch. The investigator stood and then pointed toward the trunk of a huge oak about thirty feet from the body.

Desperate to find out the fate of his niece, who might be lying only yards away from him, Steven opened his mouth to call out to Frank when the cell phone stuffed in his pocket rang.

Chapter Two

Saturday, November 8 -- 8:51 A.M.

Bobbi Cline cut across the university campus, late for a nine o'clock meeting in the auditorium. She increased her pace to a jog, eager to continue the research on her latest article for the school newspaper. The story featured a new cell phone game that had become the hottest craze on campus. After interviewing several students who had played the new game and become hooked, she decided she would attend the orientation meeting to sign-up and play in the next game.

How can I write about something if I don't experience it myself?

Although in a hurry to get to the auditorium, a pulse of light, barely noticeable at the periphery of her vision, caused her to halt and scan the area.

What was that?

Her instincts told her the distant flash, possibly originating from the woods, could not be a normal Saturday morning occurrence. For as long as she could remember, Bobbi had been able to sense when things around her appeared slightly amiss. She hoped this intuition was part of her God-given talent for investigative journalism. She knew, that more likely, she possessed a keen sense of observation and plenty of luck.

Off in the woods, behind the center field fence of the intramural softball field, Bobbi noticed a group of officials milling around. She saw intermittent flashes of white light indicating someone might be taking pictures.

From her vantage point, about a hundred yards away from the group, she could not identify the number of people in the woods or what they were doing. Stationed along the tree line and in the softball field, uniformed police officers appeared about thirty feet apart, positioned around the perimeter of the group. A steady stream of flashes, one every few seconds, emanated from the center of the action.

This must be some kind of photo shoot, maybe for a swimsuit calendar or nude modeling, she thought, *and the police are here to keep the frat boys away.*

To get a better look, she walked past the bleachers and then along the fence on the third base side of the softball field. As she eased closer to the action, she realized the photographers snapping pictures were not shooting a *Playboy College Girls of the Southeast* pictorial—she had discovered a crime scene.

Despite the warm sunshine, goose bumps formed on Bobbi's arms. She could now make out uniformed and plainclothes police officers as well as crime scene technicians working behind yellow police tape. The outfield fence and the large trees prevented her from observing specific details.

What the hell happened back there?

She took a few steps closer to get a better look when a uniformed police officer, who seemed to be only a year or two older than she was, commanded her to stop.

"What's going on over there, officer?"

"Official police business, young lady. You're going to have to move along."

Bobbi craned her neck to get a better view. "They're taking lots of pictures. Come on, what is it?"

The officer stood as tall as possible and positioned his upper body to block her view of the crime scene. When she tried to look past him, he adjusted his body position so she could not get a clear view.

"Miss, you're going to have to move along." He spread both arms out and, step by step, backed Bobbi away from the woods.

Bobbi rummaged through her backpack and pulled out her press card. "Look, I'm a member of the press." She waved the card in front of his face. "I have a right to know what is going on here."

The police officer yanked a radio out of his belt. "Sarge, this is Martin, copy?"

"Go ahead, Martin," a voice crackled back.

"I need a hand here, over." He continued backing Bobbi away from the action in the woods.

"Look, I just want to know what's going on over there," pleaded Bobbi. "I'm a reporter."

Officer Martin grabbed the press card. Studying it, he smiled and then handed it back to her. He had backed Bobbi all the way to the sidewalk behind the softball field's backstop. The police sergeant marched up behind Officer Martin and stared at Bobbi from behind mirrored sunglasses. Short and thick, the sergeant's graying number two brush cut poked out beneath the brim of his trooper-style uniform hat. He took a deep breath, expanding his barrel chest to the point of nearly popping the buttons off his shirt and grabbed the buckle of his black leather duty belt with pudgy hands.

"What do we have here, Martin?"

"She's a reporter from the campus newspaper."

Bobbi handed her press card to the sergeant. "I just want to know what's going on over there," Bobbi said, pointing to the crime scene.

The sergeant shook his head while scrutinizing her press card. "Ms. Cline, this is official police business." He held her card out. "As you may know, it is our department's policy not to comment on ongoing investigations. Seeing as you are a member of the press, you need to contact the press officer down at the station for details, which will be provided to you and your colleagues in the form of a departmental press release."

After reciting the standard press policy in a monotone voice, he looked at Officer Martin, and they exchanged smiles. "You do know who that is, the press officer, don't you?"

Bobbi snatched her card from the sergeant. "Yes, I do, and thanks for being so helpful. I stumble onto some huge crime scene, and do I get a scoop out of it? Nope. Thanks a bunch, fellas."

Still smiling, the sergeant said, "Young lady, please move along and have a nice day." The expression on his face changed from a patronizing smile to a serious look of concern. "Move the perimeter back fifty yards all the way around the scene," he said to Officer Martin.

Bobbi shaded her eyes with her hand and stared toward the crime scene in the woods behind the outfield fence. She now stood too far away to see the activity. She squinted, craning her neck in a search of further clues, but from the distance, the crime scene had vanished into the thick trees. The authorities did not want anyone else finding the now hidden crime scene.

She began pivoting to head toward the auditorium when she heard a distant sound that caused her to stop. Back near the woods, a man wearing shorts and sandals had yelled something. She squinted as the irate man gestured to a rail thin detective in a dark suit with a slight paunch. Despite the verbal barrage, the expression on the suit-man's face was stern, yet calm. He had Cuban features—a dark complexion with short black hair, graying at the temples. As he spoke, an unlit cigarette tucked into the corner of his mouth, bobbed up and down.

She strained to hear the conversation, but stood too far away from them to make out their words. The man in the shorts paced like a wild animal ready to fight. He waved his arms and glared at his companion with a rabid expression.

Even at a distance, Bobbi could tell that the man in the shorts had an athletic runner's build. He assumed a menacing stance and jabbed a finger in the other man's face. He looked familiar—short brown hair, blue eyes and handsome. After a few seconds, she recognized him as the computer professor in charge of the cell phone game she planned to write the newspaper story about. The man in the suit somehow calmed the professor, and the pair moved toward the crime scene.

Bobbi glanced at her watch.

Damn.

She took off running toward the auditorium.

How dare those cops give me the brush-off.

Although she wrote for a college newspaper, she still considered herself a legitimate member of the press. Her idols, the *Washington Post* reporters who broke the Watergate scandal, Woodward and Bernstein, would not have let the authorities push them around like that. She had just stumbled onto something big, and the police did not want her poking around. She had not observed news vans with camera crews or print guys with photographers hounding the cops. She must have been the first media person to find the scene.

Butterflies danced in her stomach. She still had a chance to scoop the mainstream media. Identifying the well-hidden crime scene, surrounded on three sides by dense woods and obscured by the outfield fence, would be difficult, *unless you were a giant center fielder.*

The thick canopy of oak trees made the area invisible from the air as well. Because of its remote location on campus and the fact that the police had extended the perimeter, it seemed unlikely the media would find out about the hidden crime scene, unless someone tipped them off. She had to find a way to get more information. A story this big could help her get a dream job with a real newspaper in a major media market, like New York, Washington or L.A.

Because she had gotten close enough to the woods to identify the activity as a crime scene, the sergeant had ordered the perimeter expanded.

The cops were definitely protecting, no, hiding, the crime scene from the public and the press.

The computer professor's name was Archer, she remembered. She had already done some preliminary investigation on him for her story. Scratching her head,

Bobbi wondered why he had rushed to the scene. His body language seemed to indicate a cross between shock and rage.

Could his wife or girlfriend be involved in whatever terrible thing had happened in those woods? Had the cops called him to the scene to identify a body? But didn't they usually do that at the morgue rather than at the actual crime scene? Maybe he had been summoned there to help the police with the case. Then why did he appear so emotional?

Unanswered questions bounced around Bobbi's mind like echoes in a cave. Seeing Professor Archer arrive at the scene gave her a leg up in breaking the story. Since the police were not giving her information, she desperately needed to talk to him. Ironically, she had already scheduled an appointment for the following week to interview him about the cell phone game for her newspaper article. Bobbi knew she could not wait until then to speak to him—she needed get to him as soon as possible.

Chapter Three

Saturday, November 8 -- 8:56 A.M.

The simultaneous ring and vibration of his cell phone startled Steven. He yanked the phone from his pocket and without waiting for the caller ID to display on the phone's screen, answered the call.

"Uncle Steven, it's Jenny. I saw that you called earlier, but you didn't leave a message. What's up?"

"Thank God you're safe." Steven's shoulders relaxed. He exhaled and looked to the sky.

Thank you, dear Lord.

"Jenny, you have no idea how good it is to hear your voice."

She laughed. "Okay, what's going on?"

"You are not going to believe my morning. I was working in my office when I got this call from—"

A hand clamped down on Steven's shoulder from behind and spun him around. Frank held his index finger to his lips while shaking his head.

"Jenny, hold on a sec." Steven covered the phone. "What the hell?"

"Tell her you'll call her back," Frank commanded.

"I'm going to tell her to get out of town."

"No, you're going to tell her that you'll call her back."

"Frank, there's a killer on the loose, and I am going to warn my niece."

"Tell her you'll call her back or so help me, Steven, I'll throw you in jail for obstructing justice. Now, tell her you'll call her back. I'm serious."

Glaring at the detective, Steven exhaled and uncovered the phone. "Jenny, you still there?"

"Yes, what—"

"Listen, I need to call you back."

"Uncle Steven, what is going on? Is everything okay?"

"Sure, I'll call you later and explain everything." He hung up the phone. "What the hell, Frank? There's a fucking murderer on the loose, and you won't let me warn my own niece?"

"Steven, listen to me."

"No, you listen to me." Steven raised his voice and jabbed his finger at Frank. "If anything happens to her you'll have to lock me up, because I swear to God—"

"Don't do it, Steven. Do *not* threaten me."

Frank's sharp tone knocked Steven back to his senses. "I'm sorry, Frank, it's just that I don't understand why I can't simply get Jenny away from here. I don't want to jeopardize this investigation, I just want to protect my family."

"I understand, but you're going to have to trust me on this."

Steven drew in a deep breath and then exhaled. "All right Frank, I do trust you. It's not like I have a choice anyhow, right?"

"No, you don't." Frank relaxed his clenched jaw and blew out a breath. "Look, all I can say right now is this case has serious visibility within the department. High level politics are involved, and the spotlight is on me to figure this mess out quickly and quietly."

Steven bit his lip, resisting the urge to press the detective further. With Jenny thankfully alive, Steven wondered why Frank had ordered him to the crime scene.

Chapter Four

Saturday, November 8 -- 8:58 A.M.

Jonathan Holden sat on the edge of the campus auditorium's stage, eyeing the partially filled rows of banked seats looming before him. He downed half a can of *Mountain Dew*, hoping the sugar and caffeine would give him a much-needed jolt. Rubbing his puffy eyes, he fought the fatigue plaguing his body. He knew the all night test-games, like the one he had played the previous night, were taking a toll on his body.

The number of students filing into the large room to hear his orientation presentation and to sign up for that night's test-game excited him. Not yet nine o'clock on a Saturday morning, and there must have been forty or fifty kids already congregating in the hall, with more streaming through the doors. You could not get him out of bed before noon on a Saturday when he had been an undergraduate student at the university. The game, *his game*, had become the hottest thing on campus.

He studied the groups of students, zeroing in on the females. It pleased him to see quite a few sorority girls in the crowd. *Not a bad crop today*, he thought, after noticing several hot young ones. His ties to the fraternities and sororities had helped him in recruiting students to play in the test-games. Although he had not been an active member of his fraternity since he had graduated a year and a half ago, he had stayed close to the Greek organizations on campus throughout the development of the game. The fraternities and sororities were leaders and trendsetters on campus, and if they got hooked on the game, other students would follow suit.

Jonathan scanned the crowd again, paying particular attention to a group of sorority girls standing toward the front of the room talking and laughing. They looked like sisters, each sporting identical bleach blonde hairstyles, waif-like model bodies and perfect smiles, which accented their gorgeous, tanned faces. One particular young blonde, however, grabbed his attention. He could not remember seeing her before—she was the type of girl that, if he *had* seen her, he would not have forgotten her.

Tall and well tanned, she wore a denim low-rise mini skirt and a white, scoop neck tank. The tiny skirt rode low on her hips and hung so short it barely served its intended purpose. Her cropped tank showed off her lean, flat stomach and pierced navel. Her natural, peach-sized breasts did not require her to wear a bra and her straight blonde hair, parted down the middle, fell over her shoulders halfway down her back. The high cheekbones, a cute button nose and a dazzling smile accentuated her runway model-like face.

Jonathan could not take his eyes off the stunning beauty. Several times during conversations with her friends, she had made eye contact with him. Normally he would have looked away, but with her, he maintained his gaze, looking straight into her deep blue eyes. A hint of mischief sparkled in those eyes. Jonathan felt butterflies in his stomach and a tingle in his loins. Fueled by a strong attraction, he began mentally undressing her.

A tap on his shoulder jolted Jonathan out of his fantasy. He jerked his head around to find Peter Vaughn standing beside him, staring at him through thick horn-rimmed glasses with eager eyes and a manufactured smile on his ugly mug.

This pain in the ass has the worst timing!

31

He predicted Peter would attempt to make small talk and try to be buddies, but Jonathan knew his ulterior motive. Peter wanted a promotion from the system administrator on the project team to software developer. Peter just did not get it. Just because you could change backup tapes, create simple scripts and install operating systems on computers, did not mean you could write software programs for them.

"Damn it, Peter."

Peter's eyebrows shot up, as he shrugged at Jonathan "What? What did I do?"

"I was just about to get to second base with…never mind. What do you want?"

"Jeez, Jonathan, I just came over to say hello. You don't have to bite my head off. God, you look exhausted."

"Yeah, well I was up all night playing in the test-game." When Peter studied him closely, Jonathan added, "What? What are you staring at? Do I have something stuck in my teeth?"

"Where did you get those scratches on your face and neck? They're all over your arms."

Jonathan's hand shot to his cheek and traced the fresh scabs on his jaw line. "It happened during the game last night. Somebody was chasing me in the thick woods on the other side of the tennis courts. It was really dark and I couldn't see a thing, so I ran right through some tree branches full of vines—you know, the kind with sharp thorns. I'm so tired I forgot about them."

"You better make sure you put something on them, or they'll get infected." Peter paused and took a breath. "So when are you gonna have some time to, you know, to talk with me about my game ideas?"

This jerk is so damned predictable. He's like a broken record.

He just could not take a hint. Jonathan did not intend to promote him to the development team.

He's just a sys admin, not a programmer.

"Peter, now's not a good time to…oh shit, here comes the bitch."

Peter's head snapped around to far right aisle leading to the stage. They watched Patricia Hunter walk toward them with a purposeful stride.

Jonathan loathed the stocky woman who stood nearly six feet tall. She had a powerful build, like that of a competitive weightlifter. Her pale, rough complexion suggested adolescent bouts with acne, and she made no attempt to cover the scars with makeup. She wore her dark hair short, almost shaved on the sides and in the back, and had it spiked up on the top with mousse, the only beauty product or cosmetic visible on her. She wore a total of five simple stud earrings, two in her left and three in her right with a miniature bolt stuck through a pierced hole at the very top of her right ear.

She leered at the group of sorority girls. Rolling her eyes and shaking her head, she breezed past them and stopped in front of Jonathan, ignoring Peter.

Leaning in, she examined his face. "What the hell happened to you? One of your sorority conquests decide to fight back last night?" She laughed.

"Fuck off." Jonathan's now crimson face featured a prominent vein centered on his forehead. "My personal life is none of your God-damned business. For your information, I was testing the game last night when—"

"Whatever, Jonathan," she said, tipping her head slightly while showing him the palm of her hand. With a quick wink and a smile that showed off the top row of her teeth, she pivoted and sauntered to the back of the room.

Jonathan burst toward her, but Peter slid into his path with his hands up. "Whoa. Hang on there, buddy. She's not worth it, just calm down."

"You're right, thanks Pete," Jonathan said in a low voice.

"Jeez, she really has it in for you," Peter said. "She's been fucking with you since the day you beat her out for the project leader job."

"Yeah, but I think she's pissed because she doesn't have a penis." They both laughed. "She thinks Archer gave me the job because I'm a guy. It's got nothing to do with gender. Bottom line—I'm the better leader, and that's why I got the job. She can say whatever she wants to me as long as she gets her job done. I can take as much of her feminist bullshit as she can dish out. She's probably a lesbian anyway."

Peter laughed again. "Jonathan, about my game ideas—"

"Listen, Peter, you better get the demo set up. We only have a few minutes until the meeting starts."

Peter's face turned a deep red. He spun and stomped toward the demo equipment. Jonathan scanned the room, hoping to find the beautiful blonde. Instead, he found himself looking directly at Patricia, who stared him down with an intense look of hatred.

Chapter Five

Saturday, November 8 -- 9:03 A.M.

Steven still had no idea why Frank had called him to the crime scene.

"Steven, I know you're upset because I made you hang up on Jenny, but you got to understand something, I'm under direct orders from the Chief himself not to discuss this case with anyone outside of our immediate investigation team. I had no choice, I've already risked my job by bringing you here."

"I just want to tell Jenny to get out of town. I promise I won't mention anything about the murder."

"Right." Frank shook his head and scrunched his brow, "And how are you going to do that? 'Hi Jenny. This is your Uncle Steven. I want you to pack up, leave school, and get out town. Why? Oh, no good reason.' Come on Steven, she ain't gonna buy that."

"What if I told her something bad happened back home, and her parents need her?"

Frank's face reddened. "Steven!"

"Alright, I understand. Why is this case such a big secret? Is it the politics you mentioned?"

"Yeah. The Chief and the president of the university are good friends. They run in the same social circles. The Chief is very sensitive about causing a panic on campus. Until we can get more evidence, our strategy is to not release any details on this case, especially details about the victim."

"So, there's a murderer loose on this campus and instead of warning potential victims, the cops are just going to sit on the information? What's the plan? Wait until the killer strikes again and again so you guys can identify a pattern? That makes no sense."

"No, it's not that simple," Frank fired back. "The department has a clear policy in these situations. We release information to the public strategically rather than broadcasting every detail we know about the case. Remember, our killer watches the six o'clock news, too, so we have to be careful about tipping our hand."

"I get that, but—"

Frank cut him off. "Exposing details too early creates panic, especially on a college campus. Chaos and panic at this early stage of the investigation causes us to lose focus. We end up using all of our investigative manpower chasing down the hundreds of bogus leads given to us by the public. To increase security, we would have to lock this campus down with virtually all the uniforms we have available, potentially leaving other parts of the city vulnerable. Right now it just doesn't make sense for us to talk publicly about the crime."

"Seems pretty risky to me." Steven tossed his hands in the air. "If another body shows up, the Chief and the department will have blood on their hands."

"Look, I'm sorry about the way I acted earlier—I know I yelled at you, and I was downright rude. If it were up to me, I would let you personally take Jenny out of town, but I've got no choice, Steven. I trust you and you are just going to have to trust me. Please do not talk about this case to anyone or I'm out of a job, okay?"

"Yeah, okay. So if Jenny's not involved, why did you ask me to come here?"

"I thought you might be able to help me out with this investigation," Frank answered, beckoning to Steven. "Follow me."

Frank led Steven over to the body. They both squatted next to the head end of the figure. Frank reached out and took hold of the white sheet. Pausing, he looked Steven in the eye. Steven gave him a nod, and Frank eased the sheet back revealing the victim's head.

Steven stared at the pretty girl's face for several seconds. Eyes wide, his jaw dropped, leaving his mouth agape. He tried to speak, but his mouth and throat felt dry, as if someone had suctioned out all of the saliva.

He swallowed hard, "Oh my God. Cover her back up."

Steven leapt to his feet and staggered a few steps away from the girl's body. He bent at the waist, resting his hands on his knees, looking as if he were about to vomit.

"What is it? Steven, do you know her?"

"Yeah...that's Christina Howard. She's Jonathan Holden's former fiancée."

"Wait a minute, who is Jonathan Holden?"

"Jonathan works for me on the cell phone game project I've been telling you about. He's the graduate student I picked to be the project leader over the development team. He was engaged to Christina for about a year and a half."

"What do you mean *was* engaged? Did they break up?"

"Yes, a couple of weeks ago."

"What happened?"

"According to Jonathan, she accused him of spending all his time working on the project. She felt neglected. She got tired of being alone every night and every weekend, so she dumped him."

"How was the break up?"

"Nasty. Jonathan is extremely bitter. He's very competitive in everything he does. When she broke off the engagement, he took it as a failure and a loss, like losing a basketball game or a tennis match. He's still pissed off about it."

"Did he try to make up with her, try to get her back?"

"Yes, he was very embarrassed when she dumped him. He tried several times to win her back—told me he just didn't understand her. He was working all these hours for them and their future, and she turns around and dumps him."

"What you do mean? Was he working all the time to save money for the wedding or a house or something?"

"Sort of, he was, and still is, working for much more than the down payment on a house or a new car. See, this project we are working on is a brand new type of game that people play on their cell phones."

"Right, you've told me a little bit about it."

"We are in the final phase of testing. This whole project is a joint effort between the university and the cellular carrier, USA Wireless. Once this thing is done, USA Wireless is most likely going to offer Jonathan a job. I mean a really good job, making big bucks. If this project is successful, and it will be, Jonathan will get a six-figure job offer along with a six-figure signing bonus and stock options to become the head of wireless game development at USA Wireless—all at the tender age of twenty-three."

"Damn, I'd be working my ass off, too."

"Right. That's why the break up was so nasty and why he's so bitter. He felt like he was busting his ass, trying to set up their future, and she couldn't see it. She put him in a no-win situation."

"Sounds to me like he was trying to do the right thing."

"Yes and no. Jonathan is one of the most dedicated and driven people I have ever worked with, almost to a fault. Even though he was telling Christina that all the long hours would end as soon as this project was finished, she knew nothing would change. Once USA Wireless hired him, there would always be "yet another project" with late nights and deadlines to meet, and the same thing would happen, again and again. Of course, he told her things would change and he probably believed it. But I know Jonathan, and she was right. He will always be the same. Work will always be his first priority. They argued about it a lot."

"You said the break up was nasty. I guess they fought?"

Steven nodded.

"Do you think it ever escalated beyond yelling?" Frank asked.

"What do you mean, like physical fighting? No," Steven answered. "Jonathan never said anything about that. He *is* very intense, and I have seen him treat people like shit, but he would never hit Christina."

"So you don't think he is capable of killing his ex-fiancée?"

"God, no. Jesus, Frank."

"Okay, take it easy. I'm just saying that from what you have told me, he has a motive. When are you going to see him again?"

"We're meeting for lunch at noon today to talk about the status of the project."

"Do me a favor, and tell me if he acts differently or weird today, okay?"

"Sure."

"And Steven, I know it will be hard, but do *not* mention Christina or anything about this case to him. I need this job. Got it?"

Chapter Six

Saturday, November 8 -- 9:07 A.M.

Steven stared at the outline of the petite body, covered by the sterile, white sheet. He silently prayed that the young woman had moved to a better place. The area where her body lay was anything but peaceful as the crime scene investigators buzzed about like flies.

He remembered meeting Christina three years before when she, a beautiful eighteen-year-old freshman, and Jonathan, first started seeing each other. The two met at a sorority rush party and she immediately fell hard for the handsome, athletic fraternity brother. They began dating and soon became inseparable.

For the next two years, a near perfect relationship ensued. Steven recalled the beaming smile Jonathan had plastered to his face as, over beers, he shared the details of his proposal to Christina. On the evening of the Fourth of July, the summer after Jonathan earned his undergraduate degree, he slipped a diamond engagement ring on Christina's hand while brilliant fireworks exploded overhead. With tears of happiness streaming down her cheeks, she had agreed to marry him. Jonathan would begin taking graduate courses in the fall. Christina planned to finish her degree in another year and after that, marriage, new careers and eventually a family.

Soon after the engagement, Jonathan accepted Steven's offer to join the cell phone game project team. Christina focused on finishing her degree and became deeply involved with her sorority, serving as an officer.

Over the years, Steven had watched as both of them blossomed and matured, transitioning from college kids into adults, and how they also began to grow apart. With Jonathan consumed by his work on the project, and Christina focused on school and her sorority duties, they saw less and less of each other. Over time, he witnessed the relationship deteriorate, eventually leading to their breakup just a few weeks before.

Steven adored Christina because she had been a good influence on Jonathan. Despite her hectic life, she tried to carve time out of her schedule for them to function as a couple. Jonathan had confided in him that several months before the break up, she had attempted to institute a weekly date night, but the weekend test-games derailed her plan. Eventually Christina stopped putting forth the effort to make Jonathan balance his priorities. Despite the nasty breakup, Steven hoped they might reconcile and get married. He forced himself to look at the sheet again—now they would never have that chance.

Steven's eyes filled with tears. He had watched Christina grow and mature into womanhood, poised to begin the next phase of her adult life. Now he could only stare at her lifeless form, her bright future doused by an unknown killer. Steven turned away from the body as a tear slipped down his cheek.

"Hey, are you okay?" Frank asked softly.

"Yeah." Clearing his throat, Steven wiped the tear away.

Christina and Jonathan's breakup had been nasty. Jonathan had told him some of the things that had been said and some of the names they had called each other during their fights. They had been brutal. However, they had also loved each other dearly for a long time.

Jonathan is not a murderer. Anyone could have committed this crime. It could have been a mugging or rape attempt gone bad, or a random act of violence by some psychopath. It's just a coincidence that Jonathan's ex-fiancée is the victim, Steven reasoned, confident he would prove that theory out when he saw Jonathan at lunch later that day.

***

Jonathan's watch read four minutes past nine—time to start the orientation meeting. He took a final look at himself in the men's room mirror. He traced his fingers over the fresh scratches on his face and neck. They did not appear too deep, *hopefully no scars*, but the newly formed red scabs stood out prominently.

He exited the bathroom and strode back into the auditorium's main hall where the students waited. A scowling Patricia stared as he dodged her and with a subtle scratch of her cheek, gave him the middle finger. He moved up the aisle toward the stage. While passing the group of sorority girls he made eye contact with the blonde. She smiled and shot him a wink. With butterflies in his stomach, caused by the wink, not nerves, he bounded onto the stage. It was show time.

Jonathan estimated eighty students now filled the auditorium, eager to hear about the cell phone game. Peter manned the laptop, connected to an LCD projector, which

47

displayed the presentation on the large screen behind the stage. Jonathan glanced at Peter, who gave him a nod.

"Would everyone please take a seat?" The crowd settled. "My name is Jonathan Holden, and I want to thank all of you for coming this morning. Let's start by doing a quick survey. Please raise your hand if you like playing video games."

Nearly every hand shot up. "Video games are fun and can be quite addictive. I'm sure I'm not the only one in this room that has missed a nine o'clock American Lit lecture because I did an all nighter on the Xbox." The crowd laughed and applauded.

"Now imagine that, instead of playing a game on a computer, you are actually playing a game against other live human players in the real world. Welcome to the WILCO Project. As you can see on the screen, WILCO is an acronym for Wireless Interactive Location-based Capture Operation. I know this name is a real mouthful… okay, it sucks." The students laughed.

"It's just the code name the project team uses for the game. We had to call it something and this is the best we could come up with." Jonathan shrugged. "We have not decided on the final, commercial name. In fact, we might have a "name the game" contest to get help from you guys to get a killer name." The crowd buzzed as students offered their opinions on potential names for the game to each other. Jonathan took a sip of his *Mountain Dew* while the crowd settled.

"The WILCO Project is an interactive game you play using your wireless phone. You play against real people in the real world. All you need to play is your USA Wireless picture phone and some friends that want to have a fun time. You can play many variations of the game, like capture the flag, team capture or sole survivor. The main theme of the game is to hunt down your enemies and eliminate them from the game by executing a capture.

Tonight's test-game, which we hope you all sign up for, is going to be team capture. The players will be divided into two teams. The object of the game is to hunt down members of the opposing team and capture them, eliminating them from the game. The team that captures all the enemy players wins the game. Each member of tonight's winning team will receive a coupon for a free lunch at Bubba's Pizza and a tee shirt courtesy of our friends at USA Wireless." The students clapped and cheered.

"First, let's talk about the hunt then I'll tell you about the capture. So how do you hunt down your enemies?

49

You use your phone. Your phone lets the game know your exact location within the game area. It is your job to use your phone to find your opponents so you can capture them.

Each of your phones has a high-resolution color display. The game has several different screens that you will use while playing. The main screen shows a zoomable map of the playing area. There is an icon representing you and each of your teammates." Jonathan held up his own phone before pressing on.

"What you *don't* see are the icons representing your opponents. In order to find your opponents, you must turn on your radar. When your radar is on, you are able to see any enemies that fall within the radar range. The radar range is limited but can be upgraded. We'll talk about upgrades later. So remember, using your radar is necessary to see where the opposing players are located on the game map.

But listen, gang, using the radar has a catch. When you turn your radar on, you can see the enemy, but likewise, the enemy can also see you. So you can search around you with your radar, but be careful because your radar also gives your position away."

A murmur of intrigue ran through the crowd. "As I mentioned just a minute ago, you can upgrade your radar with cool features. An example of one of these features is the ability to use your radar to search for the enemy in places other than your immediate vicinity. The standard radar feature works like real radar. Imagine a map with a circle on it and you positioned in the middle of the circle. You can "see" with the radar inside that surrounding circle. Wherever you move, the circle moves with you. Simple, right? The upgrade allows you to point to any place on the map and look for bad guys in that spot, regardless of your actual position. So how do you upgrade to get this and other cool features? We will get to that later." Jonathan paused and scrutinized the audience, checking for signs of boredom or disinterest. He smiled and then took a swallow of his soda.

These kids are mine. They are hooked!

"We've got the bad guy in our sights, now let's capture him. You've used your radar feature on your phone to spot an enemy. This is how to capture him and eliminate him from the game."

Jonathan yanked his phone back out of his pocket and held it for the crowd to see. He brought the phone to his eye, "Everyone say cheese!" and snapped a picture of the cheering students.

"Your USA Wireless phone is a picture phone, meaning it has a built-in digital camera. These phones are awesome because the camera is very high quality. It even has an advanced zoom feature and an unbelievable built-in LED flash."

The camera phone sported the very latest Asian technology not slated to debut in the U.S. consumer market for at least two more years. Knowing the technical details of the advanced device would be lost on the students. Steven pocketed the phone and continued his explanation.

"The way that you capture your enemy is to get close enough to take a clear picture of his or her face. Let's say you have tailed your opponent into the University Square Mall. There are tons of people shopping. How do you know which one is your enemy? Each person must wear their official team hat while they are playing."

Jonathan held up a game cap. "They are black baseball caps with Velcro removable logos on the front. You must wear your hat with your team's logo attached while you play the game.

The hats are only required if you get into a game where people do not know each other, like tonight. For example, if one fraternity, say the Pikes," a couple of students cheered, "set up a game against another fraternity, like SAE," a bigger cheer this time, "and all the players know each other, the hats are not required."

"Once you spot your opponent, you have to get close enough to take a clear picture of the player's face. The picture is transmitted back to the game immediately over the wireless network. Using sophisticated face recognition software, the game server determines if your shot was a hit or a miss.

If the image of your enemy's face is recognized successfully, then your opponent is captured, eliminated from the game. You are both notified on your phones. If you miss, that is, you were not close enough or the shot was off to the side, then only the shooter is notified of the miss."

Interest was peaking. Jonathan knew it was time to start wrapping it up.

"Finally, let's talk about those cool upgrades I mentioned earlier. Upgrades are features that can be added to the game to make it more exciting. When the game is set up, you can add what are called "upgrade spots" to the game. Just like your opponent's icons, these upgrade spots will show up on the map as radar detectable icons. That means you must use your radar to see them on the game map.

There are all kinds of these upgrades available, like upgraded radar features I have already mentioned. All you have to do to claim an upgrade is find an upgrade spot on the map and move to that location in the real world. When you get close enough you will be notified on your phone that you successfully earned the upgrade.

A good example of a cool upgrade is the long-range radar feature I described a minute ago. When your radar is upgraded with long-range capability, you can light up any remote spot on the game map with your radar. This greatly enhances your searching capabilities. Another powerful upgrade is cloaking. If you earn one of these upgrades, you become invisible to your opponent's radar for a period of time. Some cloaking upgrades start immediately. Other cloaking upgrades can be kept and turned on later when needed. Take a hint from an old WILCO Project veteran, when you see an upgrade spot, check the area closely first, then grab the sucker. Just beware of the famous cloaked ambush. So that's a very high-level look at the WILCO Project game. What do you guys think?"

Jonathan cupped his hand behind his ear and turned his head to one side. The kids broke into loud applause, complete with shouts and whistles. The audience settled. "Now we will get into some detail and then answer your questions."

Jonathan paused to take one last swig of his *Mountain Dew*. He heard comments like "Sounds like a blast!" and "This is so cool!" from the students' chatter. He smiled. He had hooked them, just like all the other groups before them.

The WILCO Project was going to be his ticket to a long and lucrative career in the business of location-based wireless gaming.

Chapter Seven

Saturday, November 8 -- 9:11 A.M.

Frank led Steven from Christina's body to the base of a large oak tree located thirty feet deeper into the woods. Steven knew Jonathan and the team should have already begun presenting the game orientation.

What if Jonathan hadn't shown up at the auditorium because he needed to get out of town real fast? No, they would have called by now—unless Patricia Hunter had filled in for him.

Jonathan had never allowed her to do the presentation at a game orientation. He would never give up the spotlight, especially to her. As second in command behind Jonathan on the project team pecking order, conducting the orientation meetings would not be an issue for her. Furthermore, she would have no problem stepping in and completely replacing Jonathan as the project leader, except for the large chip she carried around on her shoulder. She would kill to have Jonathan's job, and sometimes it seemed she wanted to do just that. Regardless, if Jonathan had gone AWOL, they would have called.

The victim's clothes, shoes, hat and a cell phone lay on the ground near the trunk of the big oak tree. The crime scene technicians had already processed the items and sealed them in clear plastic evidence bags.

"This is why I called you here," Frank said, pointing to the cell phone on the ground. "The first uniforms that responded to the scene reported that the phone was making weird noises." He stooped and picked up the phone and the hat.

"Weird noises?" Steven asked, arching his brows.

"Sounds they were pretty sure weren't ring tones. They followed crime scene protocol and did not touch the phone. After the technicians processed the phone, which was wiped clean by the way, I was able to examine it. First thing I noticed it looked like there was some kind of game playing on the screen."

Frank handed Steven the evidence bag containing the hat. Steven frowned. The black hat with a bright red "WILCO Project" logo attached to the front of it had been adjusted in the back to fit a petite head.

"Was she wearing this hat?" Steven asked.

"We don't know. The hat and the rest of her clothes were all scattered over here by this big tree."

Steven chewed his lower lip and stroked his chin. "There was a test-game conducted last night using volunteer students. If she played in the test-game, she would have been wearing the hat."

"I suspected the hat had something to do with your game project after I saw the logo. I remembered the goofy game name."

"That's just our code name, we're going to get a better one."

"So why was she wearing the hat? You guys selling merchandise already?"

Steven explained to Frank how the hat identified game players for participants that might not know each other.

"You think she was playing the game, what do you call it, Roger Wilco?"

"It's called the WILCO Project. It stands for Wireless Interactive Location-based Capture Operation."

Frank laughed. "Yeah, I know. I'm just busting your balls."

Steven smiled and shook his head. "Anyway, she may have been playing, maybe not. Let me take a look at the phone."

Steven took the phone and looked it over. "It's the same USA Wireless model we use to play the game." He flipped open the cover exposing the display window and examined the color screen through the plastic bag. Punching a couple of keys, the phone chirped a series of musical tones.

"The game is still actively running. There's no doubt about it, Frank, she *was* playing the game when she died."

Steven believed, since the police found Christina's phone with the game program active and her official black hat lying nearby, the WILCO Project played some role in the case. If Christina had not played the game, she would have no reason to venture into the woods behind the softball field late on a Friday night.

The game was responsible for Christina's death, and I'm responsible for the game.

"Oh God, Frank...I'm responsible," Steven mumbled.

"What? What are you talking about?" Frank asked.

"Was she killed in these woods?"

"We are not absolutely certain of that, but I personally would say there is a ninety-nine percent chance she died here. Probably right where the body is now."

"Don't you see? Playing the game got her into these woods. The game was...I don't know, an enabler."

"Are you trying to say that if she hadn't played the game last night, she never would have been in these woods and would still be alive today?"

"That's right."

"And you feel that makes you responsible?"

"I *am* ultimately responsible for the WILCO Project. If I had never created the game, Christina would be alive today, and you and I would be sipping *Amstel Lights* and watching the football game this afternoon instead of trying to solve her murder."

"Maybe that's true and maybe it's not, but listen to me, neither you nor the game killed this girl. Some sick asshole, for whatever reason, killed Christina."

"But, if it weren't for the game..."

"Then by your logic, Henry Ford and the Wright brothers are mass murderers because thousands of people die each year while riding in cars and planes. Christ, for being so smart, you sure are dumb sometimes."

"But—"

"But nothing. Stop feeling sorry for yourself and help me find the monster that really did this."

***

Nearly every student who listened to Jonathan's orientation presentation stood in line to sign up for that night's test-game. Jonathan glanced at his watch, noting it was almost eleven o'clock. The presentation and question and answer session had lasted nearly two hours. Patricia, Peter and a few others from the project team manned tables in the back of the room, signing up the students. He noticed Andy Perkins, the product-marketing guy from USA Wireless, striding toward him—he was right on time for their appointment to explain and demonstrate the player sign-up process.

"Andy, good to see you again," said Jonathan, greeting him with a big smile and pumping his outstretched hand.

"Hi Jonathan. I'm looking forward to understanding the sign-up process. We have got to make sure the commercial launch of the game is simple and smooth."

Commercial launch—this is getting real.

Butterflies of excitement fluttered in Jonathon's stomach as he led Andy to a table.

"The first step is to get the player to sign the phone damage agreement," said Jonathan as he handed Andy a blank form from the box. "As you can see here, the player is agreeing to assume responsibility for the cost of a lost or damaged cell phone. If something happens to the phone, you guys directly bill the student's university account for the cost."

Andy nodded and scratched a note on his pad. "Yeah, these handsets are state of the art and not cheap. I'll need to have legal revise this form for general consumer use. I don't see a problem. What's next?" he asked.

"Now we have the student swipe their university ID, which is a smart card that uses an embedded Java chip, through that card reader attached to the laptop," said Jonathan. "Most of the data we need from the student is stored on their ID so there is minimal data entry."

"Nice," replied Andy. "And more importantly, fast and efficient."

"Yeah, move 'em through," said Jonathan with a smile. "Next, the registration program on the laptop creates a record on the WILCO Project game server located in our data center across campus. We encrypt the data and send it over the campus-wide WiFi network."

"So you have already addressed user data security, good." Andy scrawled another quick note. "We'll want to run a standard security audit. Any issue with that?"

"Not at all," replied Jonathan. "Just shoot me an email when you want to get that scheduled. Now, take a look on the laptop screen. See how the player's information record is now displayed? All we do next is add the last few fields of information, and the player is in the system."

"Very cool," replied Andy. "I see the student's picture already displayed. Is that pulled from the ID card?"

"Correct. The game uses that picture for the face recognition. Most of the pictures from the ID cards are fine, but once in awhile the program will kick the picture back— might be too dark or too small. In that case, we just snap a new head shot right here and it goes right into the database."

"What's next?" asked Andy.

"Just a couple more steps," answered Jonathan. "First, the player picks a unique user name and password that they will use to log in to the game's website. Then, we grab a phone, fire it up and record the unique ESN identifying number from the handset into the database record."

"So you use the phone's ESN number in the game's database to link the phone to the player?" asked Andy.

"That's right," replied Jonathan. "That enables us to track the player's movement in the game via the phone. Next, we ask the player to sign the liability forms, then activate the phone and hand it to the player along with the official hat."

Andy grabbed a hat and chuckled. "Any progress on a final name for the game? Because the WILCO Project sucks."

Jonathan laughed. "I know. If I had a dollar for every time someone made fun of our code name I would be a rich man."

"Something tells me that whatever you end up calling this thing, you're going end up a rich man. Great job so far, and I look forward to working with you," said Andy, and he gave Jonathan a wink.

They shook hands, and Jonathan smiled as he watched Andy walked out of the room.

Jonathan sat on the edge of the stage and yawned as the excitement of the presentation and the successful meeting with Andy wore off. He spotted the stunning blonde standing in Peter's line, next to sign up.

That ugly looking geek will probably cream his jeans when she bends down to sign her forms.

A tall brunette with long, dark hair pulled back into a single braid approached Jonathan. She wore large glasses with thick dark frames that had gone out of style in the late eighties. Her pretty face featured a smooth complexion showing no traces of make-up. Baggy clothes hid the details of her tall, slender frame, but Jonathan could see enough to determine she had been blessed with a nice figure.

All this girl needs is a fashion makeover and LASIK surgery and she could be a model.

"Hi Jonathan, I'm Bobbi Cline. I write for the school newspaper. Great presentation!"

"Thanks. You sign up yet?"

"Sure did. Going to give it a try tonight. Speaking of the game, I'm doing a story on the WILCO Project game for the paper."

"Right, now I recognize your name. You're interviewing Professor Archer next week. He asked me to join you two."

"That sounds great. Have you spoken to Professor Archer today?"

"No, why do you ask?" Jonathan shot her a quizzical look.

"I think I saw him earlier—never mind. Nice meeting you, and if I don't run into you playing tonight, I'll see you next week for the interview." She whirled and hustled toward the exit.

Scratching his chin, Jonathan wondered why she had asked him about Professor Archer. After he'd answered the question, her demeanor changed. Her confidence turned to nervousness, and she had not been able escape the conversation fast enough.

Jonathan yawned again and looked toward Peter's table, hoping to catch another look at the blonde. Expecting her to be finished signing up for the game and gone, warmth washed over his body when he spotted her still talking to Peter. Bent down with her hands flat on the table leaning toward Peter, she threw her head back and laughed as if he had just told the funniest joke she had ever heard. A huge grin stretched across Peter's face—he certainly was enjoying her company.

Jonathan gazed at her long, brown legs, beginning from her feet and moving all the way up to her barely covered rear end. Her flawless body sent a tingle of desire snaking through his body again.

The blonde stood straight, holding her new phone and hat, while continuing her conversation with Peter.

Surely, they weren't just chatting. What is that nerd trying to do, pick her up? Like that fat, greasy troll has a shot in hell with her.

They continued talking while the other kids in line behind her frowned and glanced at their watches. Some jumped out of Peter's line, switching to shorter lines.

Jonathan frowned.

Great. The frog is trying to kiss the princess.

He hustled to Peter's table.

"Peter, is there a problem?"

"No, I was just—"

"Aren't you going to introduce me to your friend?" He did not wait for Peter to reply and turned to the blonde. "I'm Jonathan. Sorry about Peter keeping you here, sometimes he talks too much." He turned back to Peter, whose face had turned a deep red. "Thanks Pete, I'll take it from here. Go ahead and get the next person."

Speechless, Peter frowned at Jonathan who winked at him and escorted the blonde away from the sign-up tables.

"I hope he wasn't pestering you," Jonathan said.

"No, I was just asking him some questions about playing the game."

"Well, you're looking at the expert. I'm in charge of game development, so you can ask me anything you want about it. But first, you have to tell me your name."

"I'm Amanda Harvey." She smiled and extended her hand. As her hand touched his, another tingle worked its way down his spine.

"Amanda, it's a pleasure to meet you. So what do you think about my game?"

"It looks like fun. I can't wait to play tonight. Some of my friends have already played and they love it."

"Excellent."

"It just looks like, a little complicated for someone like me. You know, like cloaking and radar, I don't know anything about that stuff."

"I can understand how you might think it's complicated, but it's really not. Trust me. I'll tell you what, if you want, I'll give you a private lesson on how to play the game. I can teach you all the tricks. I'm free after lunch today."

"I would love to, but I think I'm supposed to see a movie with a friend—a girlfriend."

68

"Cancel on her. You can see a movie anytime. You'll enjoy playing the game much more if you learn all the tricks first. Why don't we meet this afternoon?"

"Would it be like a date?" She raised her eyebrows and flashed a perfect smile.

"It can be if you want it to be." Jonathan smiled back at her, pleased with the direction the conversation had turned.

"Aren't you engaged to that Tri Delt, Christina?"

"No, we broke up a couple weeks ago," Jonathan answered, shrugging.

Damn it, they must have announced the break up at freshman orientation.

"I'm sorry, I heard you guys were together forever."

"Yeah, but it's for the best. Christina and I are moving in different directions. I've got a lunch appointment, so how about we meet in my office at the computer center, about one-thirty?"

"Okay, sure. See you there." She turned to go then looked back at him. "What happened to your face? Did you get in a fight or something?"

Jonathan's face flashed pink, and his hand darted to his jaw. "Uh, no, nothing like that. I scratched myself playing the game last night, no big deal."

Amanda flipped around to face him again. "Oh," she said, her mouth twisting into a frown. "I didn't know the game was like, violent."

"No, no. The game is not like that." He pointed to the cuts on his jaw. "These are my own fault. It was dark, and I ran through some trees. No big deal."

Amanda pursed her lips. "You poor baby." She touched her index finger to her lips and then tapped Jonathan's cheek. "See you after lunch." She twirled around and walked out.

He may have been out of circulation for a while, but he still had the old "Golden Holden" charm. He was not sure who had been flirting more, him or Amanda. Confident women turned him on. *Speaking of turn on,* Jonathan put one hand on top of the other and held them in front of his crotch.

"You just can't keep your paws off the fresh meat, can you?"

Jonathan spun around to see Patricia, arms crossed, scowling at him.

"Weren't you committed to spend the rest of your life with Christina just a few short days ago? Oh yeah, I forgot, she dumped you. I don't blame her a bit. Now you just cruise around this campus, sport fucking every sorority girl with a pulse. You are a pathetic, womanizing pig."

Without waiting for a response, Patricia whirled and stomped out of the auditorium.

Chapter Eight

Saturday, November 8 -- 12:10 P.M.

At ten minutes past noon Steven rushed through the door of *Thom Phoolery's*, a sport's bar and college hangout located just off campus. He paused at the vacant hostess stand and surveyed the sparse lunch crowd.

This place is dead—for now anyway.

Later, the entire restaurant and double bars would be jammed with drunk, screaming college students, all eyes glued to the numerous TV's placed throughout the establishment, rooting for the university's football team. This week they would be playing a road game against a tough conference rival.

Steven spotted his project manager, Jonathan, slumped in a booth at the back, head bowed as if in another world. Adrenaline tracking through his veins, Steven's pulse rate jumped, and he forced a deep breath. Drying his palms on his shirttail, he hustled over, slid into the seat across from him and slapped him on the shoulder.

"Jonathan, how'd it go last night? What the hell happened to you?" Steven stared at Jonathan's face. A good-looking kid, the girls went crazy over his blonde hair, blue eyes and athletic body. He looked more like a California surfer than a computer nerd, but the fresh scratches on his right cheek marred his handsome face. Steven also noticed similar scratches on his neck and arms.

"What? Oh, the scratches. Man, I keep forgetting about them."

"Did you get in a fight or something?"

"I sure did." Jonathan laughed. "I got tangled up with a gang of thorny vines that tried to teach me a lesson last night. I was playing in the test-game, chasing someone in those woods on the edge of campus."

"Out by the intramural fields?" asked Steven. He flashed back to the vision of Christina's sheet-covered body lying in the woods, and his guts twisted into a knot.

"Yeah. So it's pretty dark and I'm running along looking down at my phone and scanning the radar. That's when I see the enemy player changing direction, trying to get out of the woods. I tried to bust through the tree line to cut him off, and the next thing I know, I'm all tangled in vines—you know, the kind with sharp thorns."

"Those cuts look pretty bad," Steven said, tracing his own cheek with his fingertips. Vines in the woods might have scratched Jonathan, or maybe Christina fighting off his attack had caused the cuts. A wave of nausea swept over him.

"You look a little pale, are you okay?"

Before Steven could answer, the waitress arrived. They both ordered *Cokes*, Steven diet and Jonathan regular.

"Did you get her?" Steven asked. A dangerous question, but Steven took a chance and fished for information. It worked in the movies all the time—the detective trips up the suspect with a well-timed, unanticipated leading question.

"Huh? Get her? What are you talking about?"

"Last night?"

"Oh, you mean the other guy in the game last night in the woods?" Jonathan laughed. This was no Hollywood production, and he had not taken the bait. "No, by the time I got untangled from the vines, the bad guy was gone."

The waitress dropped off their drinks.

"Everything else go okay with the test-game?" Steven asked.

74

"As far as I know, the software worked like a charm. The game is ready for prime time."

"How did the orientation go this morning?"

"Good and bad. The good news is about eighty students showed up. It looked like almost all of them signed up for the test-game tonight."

"That's great."

"Yeah, the game is really taking off. I knew once I got the fraternities going, everything else would fall into place."

"You mentioned some bad news?"

"Oh, yes." Jonathan furrowed his brow, and the corners of his mouth dipped. "I've got to come clean with you on something I did." Jonathan looked down at the table and paused for a few seconds. "There's something I need to tell you."

"What is it?" A fresh batch of adrenaline revved Steven up.

"I had a pretty nasty run-in with Patricia in the auditorium this morning."

"Oh?" Steven, realizing he had been holding his breath, exhaled in relief.

Thank God.

He could deal with a petty argument much better than a murder confession.

"Yeah, I'm really sorry. I shouldn't let her get to me."

"What happened?"

"You've got to understand, I was exhausted from playing the game all night, and—"

"Jonathan, just tell me what happened."

"Okay, sorry. Right before I was about to start the presentation, she came up to me with her usual attitude. She saw the scratches on my face and neck and made some comment like 'Did one of your sorority girls fight back last night?' I don't know what happened to me, I kind of lost it and told her to…to fuck off."

"Damn it." Steven shook his head and bit his lip. "What else was said?"

"That's it, really. I tried to explain about the thorny vines in the woods, but she blew me off and walked away."

"Jesus, Jonathan! You can't let her get under your skin like that. I wouldn't put it past her to be documenting all these little incidents for a sexual discrimination lawsuit. A lawsuit like that would kill the project along with your chances for the job at USA Wireless."

"I know, and I'm really sorry. It's just that she pushed my buttons, and I went into some kind of rage. It was like for a split second I had no control."

Steven fidgeted with his silverware. Christina had pushed Jonathan's buttons during their relationship—many times during their frequent arguments. Had Christina said something to Jonathan last night causing him to lose control?

"Jonathan, the reason I picked you over her to run this project is your leadership abilities. Part of that is dealing with situations like this. This is a classic case of a disgruntled employee. When I was in the private sector, I had to deal with these things all the time.

Steven tossed his hands in the air. "It's obvious Patricia feels slighted because she didn't get the job she wanted, your job. She feels she is capable and deserving. What makes this situation more difficult is that, from a pure job performance perspective, she *is* capable of being the project leader. In fact, she is just as capable as you are."

Steven paused and sipped his drink. "What she doesn't have is the ability to be a leader in times of adversity. Leaders have passion for their work, but they don't let emotions cloud their judgment. Patricia does great work, but she is just too emotional. We all see it in her behavior. She thinks she lost the project leader job because she is female, but she didn't get it because she is too emotional, and she has a chip on her shoulder."

Nodding, Jonathan sighed.

"Don't let her get to you. Rise above her emotion and be the leader that you can be. That's why I chose you."

"You're right." Jonathan's shoulders slumped, and he stared at the table, unwilling to look Steven in the eye." I'm really sorry."

"It's okay, this is a learning experience. We just can't afford to get sued. Try not to react emotionally to her. She is baiting you and trying to get you to do something you'll regret." Steven offered him a smile. "I'm glad you told me what happened. I'm going to have a talk with Patricia about her attitude and ask her to be more professional."

The waitress arrived with drink refills and asked if they were ready to order. Steven told her they were waiting for another person to join them.

"Hershman's late again," Jonathan said, shaking his head in disgust.

"Give the poor guy a break, it's the weekend."

"He's probably still recovering."

Steven arched his eyebrows and cocked his head.

"I'll bet Patricia wore him out after they got home from the game last night."

"What?" Steven asked, his mouth hanging open. "What the hell are you talking about?"

"Come on, everybody knows they've been getting it on. She tries to hide it, but it's pretty obvious."

Shaking his head, Steven laid his hands on the table. Larry Hershman, the USA Wireless project manager assigned to work on the WILCO Project, had to be close to fifty years old.

Patricia's got to be half his age.

"I had no idea," Steven said, shrugging his shoulders.

"They spent a lot of late nights together working on the interface between the USA Wireless computer and our game server. I guess one thing led to another."

"You know, Larry just got divorced about six months ago."

"Yeah, wife number two left him high and dry."

"Between you and me, I wasn't sure Patricia was interested in dating men." Steven bit his lip.

Shouldn't have let that one slip, damn it.

79

"Apparently she does, so now everyone thinks she's a switch hitter. Somebody said she likes to use a strap-on and pitch while Hershman catches."

Steven winced.

Jonathan continued, "I heard Hershman's into that kinky domination stuff."

Patricia certainly has a dominating personality, and Larry's a strange guy all right, but I never figured him for the masochistic sort.

Steven imagined a leather-clad Larry Hershman on all fours with Patricia Hunter behind him, sporting a male strap-on device, smiling wickedly, poised to mount. *Gross.* He shook the vision out of his mind.

Patricia would probably enjoy dishing out that kind of punishment to any man. He guessed that with Jonathan winning the project leader job, she would really enjoy hog tying him and doing some serious damage to him from behind. Steven tried unsuccessfully to stifle a chuckle.

"What's so funny?" Jonathan asked.

"Nothing, I was just thinking." Steven caught someone approaching the booth out of the corner of his eye. "Here comes Larry, behave."

Steven and Jonathan exchanged smiles as Larry slid into the booth next to Steven.

"Sorry I'm late," Larry mumbled.

On cue, the waitress hustled to the table to take their lunch orders. While Jonathan ordered his food, Steven's cell phone rang. The caller ID showed Frank's number. He answered and asked the detective to hold on. After ordering a cup of soup, citing an upset stomach, he excused himself from the table. Slipping off to an empty section, far enough away that the other two could not hear him, he took Frank's call.

"How's it going with your boy?" Frank asked.

"He seems pretty normal emotionally. He had a spat with one of the developers on the team this morning, but that's not unusual. There is something else though."

"What?"

"He's got these scratches. They're on his face and neck and arms."

"Bingo. What did he say about them?"

"He said he ran into some thorny vines in the woods while playing the game last night."

"He got the scratches from vines in the woods? Did he say what woods?"

"Yeah." Steven tried to swallow but his throat had become dry. "The woods by the intramural fields."

81

"Bingo, again. Do they look like scratches from thorny vines?"

"Yes, they do."

"Okay, let's try this a different way. Do they look like they could be related to this morning's situation?"

"I don't know, Frank."

"Come on, help me out here. Is there a possibility?"

"Maybe, I don't know for sure. Okay, yes, there is a possibility they could be related."

"Got it. Anything else I should know about?"

"No."

"Thanks. Oh yeah, I've got a question for you. Something's come up that we can't explain, and I thought maybe you could help. We looked at the "dialed numbers" log on the victim's phone we found. It shows she called 911 at twelve-fifteen this morning. We checked with the 911 response center, and their log shows that the call came in, but it was a hang up."

"You mean she dialed 911 and then hung up?"

"That's right. She never talked to a 911 operator."

"That's strange. Why would she dial 911 and then not ask for help?"

"Not sure, and it gets stranger. You know what E-911 is?"

"Sure, it's Enhanced 911. It's where the 911 operator is automatically given the location of where the 911 call is made."

"Right, well our victim—"

Steven interrupted, knowing what Frank was about to say. "She was using the USA Wireless network which supports E-911."

"That's right. So the 911 operator gets the call from the victim who then hangs up. Following proper procedure, the operator immediately dispatches a patrol car to the location on the computer where the call was dialed."

"That's how you found her. I was wondering who found the body."

"No. That's *not* how we found the body. A guy from the maintenance crew mowing the intramural field decides to take a leak in the woods, spots the body and then reports it."

"Before the patrol car got there? Why were they mowing the field in the middle of the night?"

"No. The body wasn't found until early this morning."

"Frank, I'm lost. The police were dispatched to the location right after midnight. Are you saying that they weren't the ones that found the body? It was a mowing crew this morning?"

"That's right. That is what is baffling us. The patrol car wasn't sent to the university, it was dispatched to the Town Center Mall parking lot."

"What? That's thirty miles away from where Chri—, I mean the victim was found."

"Bingo. Any ideas?"

"Got to be some bug in the E-911 system."

"Steven, can you see what you can come up with on that?"

"Sure thing."

"I've got to go, but I wanted to give you a heads up on something. I had to brief the Chief himself a few minutes ago. It turns out the Chief and the president of the university are golfing buddies."

"So that's why this case is being kept so hush-hush."

"That's part of it. Anyway, I had to tell the brass you were involved in the investigation."

"I thought they weren't supposed to know that. Did you get into any trouble?"

"They were pissed at first because I brought you onto the crime scene without authorization. But then they forgot they were mad when I explained that you might be able to help us explain the erroneous location data of the 911 call."

"So you're not in trouble?"

"No, but you might get a little heat. I had to tell them the victim was playing your game at the time of the incident. I hope I'm wrong, but I'm afraid the Chief might say something about it to the president because of their friendship. The shit might roll downhill and hit you. Aren't you having troubles with some dean over there at the university?"

"Yes, you could say that," answered Steven. "Ever since that little prick Herbert took over as the acting dean, he's been gunning for me."

"What do you mean, like, trying to get you fired? I don't get it, you're a great professor."

"Well that isn't necessarily good enough for Herbert. Since I don't have the letters P-H-D behind my name, he doesn't think I am qualified."

"That's straight-up bullshit," said Frank.

"I know, but he is on a mission to get rid of all non-academics like me, and he darn near convinced the university to not renew my contract last year. Thank God my department head had my back."

"Well, shit. If this game of yours ends up mixed up in this case, that would give this pompous asshole more ammunition against you, wouldn't it?"

"Yeah, I'm not going to worry about that snob, Herbert, but I appreciate the heads up," Steven said, trying to sound tough.

"Listen, I've got to run, but I still need to talk with you about the location of the 911 call."

"Sure, can you meet me in my office at one-thirty?" Steven asked.

"I'll be there."

Chapter Nine

Saturday, November 8 -- 12:19 P.M.

Steven stared across the restaurant at Jonathan. The scratches on his face, neck and arms could certainly be the result of a physical struggle with Christina. Jonathan, who Steven estimated to be about six feet, two inches tall and probably weighed in at around two hundred and ten pounds, would easily be capable of overpowering a petite girl like Christina. That did not mean Christina could not inflict some damage though, especially if she were fighting for her life.

Steven did not like Frank's replies of "bingo" after hearing about Jonathan's scratches. His tone implied he already knew about the injuries and had been waiting for Steven to verify their existence. It seemed Frank, without directly saying it, had deemed Jonathan the prime suspect in the case.

Frank must have possessed more detailed information about the case than he had divulged to Steven. Although the killer had wiped the fingerprints from Christina's cell phone, perhaps detectives had discovered other evidence at the crime scene that pointed to Jonathan.

Were the scratches the confirming piece of evidence Frank needed to make a case against Jonathan? Had an autopsy already been completed on Christina? Perhaps they had found skin or traces of blood underneath her fingernails. The police had not even questioned Jonathan, let alone asked him for DNA samples.

Steven recalled an article he had recently read about how the Florida Department of Law Enforcement had compiled a criminal DNA database. FDLE collected DNA samples from all suspects arrested in Florida and catalogued them in a centralized database housed in Tallahassee.

Could Jonathan have a prior criminal record? DUI? Shoplifting? What if the police had previously arrested Jonathan and Steven had not known about it? Could the police have already taken DNA evidence, processed it and matched it to Jonathan?

No. Steven shook his head. He would have known if the cops had arrested Jonathan in the past couple of years, considering they had spent most of their waking hours working closely together. Also, there was no way the coroner could have possibly performed an autopsy already.

Steven knew Jonathan did have a temper, but he employed words as his weapon of choice, not his fists. When he lost his temper, he never resorted to physical violence, like earlier that morning with Patricia at the game orientation presentation where by his own admission he "kind of lost it." He had not shoved or punched her, he swore at her. No, Jonathan was not a violent person.

Next, Steven considered that the maintenance crew had found the body in the woods. If Jonathan had killed Christina, how had he lured her there to kill her? Frank had seemed almost positive the killer had murdered her in the woods where the crew had found the body. Had Jonathan met her somewhere and then forced her into the woods? Playing the game was an intense experience requiring concentration. It would be unusual for a player to agree to meet someone while in the midst of playing a WILCO Project game.

He could not figure out how Jonathan might have lured the victim unless he had possibly called her and told her he was in some sort of trouble in the woods and needed her help. Even then, if she had agreed to help him, she would have probably taken a friend or at least asked someone to meet her there rather than venturing alone to such a desolate area of campus. A killer would not risk inviting the victim and a witness to the scene of the crime.

The apparent incorrect E-911 data baffled him. How could the location of the 911 call from Christina's phone have been off by thirty miles? The location data was not infallible, but an error of that magnitude just seemed odd.

Although he needed to remain focused on the problem with the E-911 data, Steven worried that the case might cause him further problems with Dr. Herbert. Steven had tried to appear tough to Frank, as though he could care less about the acting dean, but Steven loved his job, and he did not want to lose his position at the university. Teaching was fun and satisfying, and he knew he was good at it. He decided not to worry about Dr. Herbert and focus on helping Frank with the case.

Scratching his chin, he decided his next move was to figure out why the E-911 location data from Christina's phone had been incorrect.

Steven rubbed his eyes, his brain exhausted from analyzing the morning's events. He took a couple of deep breaths and listened to the classic *Bachman Turner Overdrive* hit pumping out of the restaurant's sound system.

Closing his eyes, he allowed his mind to clear. He focused on the words of the song's refrain as the singer belted out the theme of taking care of business.

After several seconds, he opened his eyes and surveyed the sports memorabilia covering the walls, feeling energized. There had been a tragedy on campus he had unwittingly been thrust into, and the time had come for him to step up and take care of business before the killer struck again.

***

That afternoon, Jonathan heard a knock on his office door in the campus computer center. Anticipating Amanda's entrance, the butterflies he had experienced when they met in the auditorium earlier that morning made a return trip to his stomach.

"Come in," Jonathan said loudly. The door opened, and Amanda Harvey glided into his office. She wore the same outfit she had on that morning and somehow looked even sexier. Jonathan stood and swung around from behind his desk to greet her.

"Hi," she said, smiling and glancing around. "Cool office."

"Thanks, it's okay I guess."

"So, this is where you work. Like, what exactly do you do here?"

"Please, sit down." Jonathan pointed to the chair opposite his desk. Despite her extremely short skirt, Amanda managed to sit gracefully in the chair without flashing her panties. Jonathan returned to his chair behind his desk. "I am the project leader for the WILCO Project game development team."

"So what does that mean?"

"I manage the entire staff of software developers that are designing, writing and testing the programs that make up the game."

"That sounds important."

"It's a big responsibility. But enough about my boring job. Where are you from?"

"I'm from Palm Beach, my parents live there."

"Palm Beach, sounds swanky."

"Daddy's rich. He's like the largest real estate developer in the county." She pulled her shoulders back, showing off her exquisite chest. "I'm daddy's innocent little girl."

Seeing how far he could take it, Jonathan said, "I think you're a naughty girl. Does the naughty girl need a spanking?"

Jonathan half expected her to slap him across the face and storm out of his office, but instead, she flashed a wicked smile and fired back, "Promises, promises."

Jonathan swallowed hard. He did not know whether to jump over the desk and rip her clothes off or bolt out of the office and run as fast and as far as he could. Trying to be cool, he replied, "We'll talk about that later. So, this is your first semester here, right?"

"Yeah."

"You were hanging with Kappa Thetas at the meeting this morning. Are you pledging?" Jonathan asked.

"Yep. I'm a legacy. Both Granny Emma and mommy were Thetas."

"You know, I was the president of SAE my senior year."

"Wow, that's so cool. I'm just hoping to survive this pledging stuff." Her lips puckered into a pout. "If I have to like parade down fraternity row in my pajamas one more time…"

Jonathan visualized her perfect body in a skimpy, red Victoria Secret number. "It sucks because I like to sleep in the nude." Her flirty smile returned.

"Really?"

Damn, she is sexy, but it's time to dial it back down again.

"Let me go ahead and show you how the game works, and then we'll plan a pajama party."

Jonathan started up a Web browser on his computer screen and opened up the WILCO Project website. He explained the basic game functions and how they worked on the cell phone.

"See, I told you it wasn't that complicated." Jonathan smiled.

"You're right. It really looks like fun."

"Oh, there's one more thing I want to show you about the radar." He pointed to a small icon on his computer monitor.

"I can't see it very well," she said. She stood and then eased behind Jonathan. Placing her hands on his shoulders, she bent down with her lips not quite touching his ear. Goose bumps broke out across his entire body. He inhaled her sweet scent, accented by expensive perfume and felt her warm breath on his neck and in his ear.

"Are you talking about that?" she asked, leaning across his body and pointing to a spot on the screen, her breast lightly brushing his shoulder. Lightning bolts of desire struck through his body. Turning his head to look back at her, he inadvertently swiveled his chair into her legs causing her to lose her balance and fall into his lap.

"Amanda, are you okay?" He scanned her face. Eyes pinched shut, she lay motionless in his arms. Then she burst out laughing.

"I'm fine." She laughed harder and pointed her index finger at his nose. "You should have seen the look on your face."

"Why, you little faker." He smiled and tickled her ribcage until she screamed for him to stop.

"Jeez, can you keep it down in there? Some of us are trying to work," boomed a voice from outside the office.

This ignited another laughing spell, which they tried unsuccessfully to suppress. Peter Vaughn jabbed his head into the office and glared at Jonathan holding Amanda closely in his lap, both still giggling.

"What the—? Oh, hi, Amanda."

"Hi, it's Peter, right?" she answered.

"Peter, do you mind? We're kind of in the middle of something here," Jonathan interrupted, shooting a cross look at Peter.

Peter's face turned crimson. Without replying, he wheeled around and fled the office, slamming the door shut behind him.

This kicked off another fit of laughter. After regaining their composure, Jonathan began caressing Amanda's bare shoulder. Their eyes met and they shared a brief, soft kiss.

Amanda pulled back, taking a deep breath.

"Wow," she gasped and popped out of Jonathan's lap, face flush.

Jonathan stood and faced her. "I have an idea. Let's have dinner tonight before the game."

"I'd love to," she replied, offering him a warm smile. "Well, I'd better go, pledge stuff, you know."

They agreed to have dinner at Jonathan's favorite restaurant, a small family-owned Italian place located just off campus. He gave her a hug, and she opened the door and slipped out of the office. Exhausted and knowing he would be up most of the night, Jonathan quickly checked his email and then headed to his apartment to take a nap.

Chapter Ten

Saturday, November 8 -- 1:27 P.M.

Steven approached the entrance to the campus computer center. He spotted Frank waiting by the glass doors, sucking on a cigarette and talking on his cell phone. When the detective spotted Steven, he nodded and ended his call. After a final drag on his cigarette, he flicked the butt away, and they shook hands.

"Steven, how are you holding up?"

"I'm fine. Any new information?"

"Not here, upstairs in your office, my friend."

They entered the building and climbed the stairs to Steven's second floor office. Once inside, Steven closed the door behind them and motioned Frank to a chair by the door. Frank slumped into the chair while Steven sat behind his desk. Thick bags of loose skin, tinted slate-grey, sagged under his dark chocolate eyes. He reeked of sweat and nicotine.

"Frank, are you sure the location reported by the E-911 system last night was the Town Center Mall?"

"Damn sure—we double checked the logs. The operator dispatched the patrol unit to the east parking lot of the mall."

"I know you told me this morning that the murder was committed in the woods, but is it at all possible she was killed at the mall and her body dumped in the woods on campus?"

"Anything is possible, but the evidence strongly suggests she was killed in the woods where we met this morning."

"What evidence?"

Frank glanced at the closed office door then turned back to Steven.

"This is highly confidential. It must not leave this room, understand?"

"Sure."

"We are almost certain Christina was killed by strangulation. We've determined there was a struggle between her and the killer right in the area of the woods where the body was found. That's where she died. What we don't know is, how a 911 call from her phone could have been placed thirty miles away. Do you know how the E-911 stuff works?"

"Yes," said Steven. "You already know that the ability for operators in a PSAP to have location data show up on their computer screen for incoming 911 calls is known as enhanced 911, or E-911."

"I know what E-911 is, but what's a PSAP?"

"That's an acronym for Public Safety Answering Point. That's just a generic name for the place where the 911 operators answer the emergency calls and where all the equipment is housed. You know, the computers and phone switches."

"Okay, so how does E-911 really work?" Frank demanded.

"Anytime a person dials 911 from a regular landline phone, the location of the phone is reported to the PSAP operator—the address just pops up on the computer screen. This is not necessarily the case for cell phones."

Frank said, "So a person using their cell can call 911, but the location might not be available to the operator."

"Correct. Some wireless networks have E-911 capabilities, some do not."

"How come?" asked Frank, shrugging his shoulders.

"It really depends on how sophisticated a carrier's network is. Remember when you got your first cell phone years ago? It was a huge thing the size of a brick and most calls had all kinds of static and were dropped."

"I remember," Frank chuckled. "And you paid a fortune for that crappy service."

"That's right," said Steven. "Those early networks were analog or first-generation. Now, all the wireless carriers have digital, 3G networks, which combine voice and data. This is what allows us to do cool things like get email and surf the internet on our cell phones. 3G networks also provide LBS capability, or location-based services. LBS is the technology used to provide the E-911 data to the PSAP."

"But not all wireless companies have this LBS capability?" guessed Frank.

"Not yet. The federal government has mandated that all wireless carriers upgrade their networks to provide E-911 data to PSAP locations in the next couple of years. Also, just because a wireless carrier has LBS on their network, it doesn't mean E-911 is implemented in a given area."

"What do you mean?" Frank asked, scrunching his eyebrows.

"Not only does the carrier's wireless network have to support LBS, but there must be the proper equipment and software at the PSAP to handle the location data. An agreement between the carrier and the PSAP must also be in place."

"So I gather USA Wireless supports all this 3G and LBS stuff."

"Right," said Steven. "The LBS data used for E-911 is the same data we use for our game."

"Hold on, so you use the same location data for your cell phone game that is used for E-911 location data?"

"That's right. That's how we keep track of where all the players are located when playing the game. The LBS data from USA Wireless is the basis for the radar feature, which is how the players search for their opponents."

"So without getting too deep, how does the wireless network know the actual location of the phones?" Frank wondered.

"There are a couple of different techniques. You know that a wireless network is made up of a whole bunch of cell towers, right? Using signal strength to determine distance from the towers, computers on the network use software programs to triangulate the exact location of each cell phone."

"Yeah, makes sense."

"Okay, that's one technique. The other technique uses satellite GPS," said Steven.

"The same technology used by all these new car navigation systems?"

"Right. Some wireless phones actually have GPS chips built into them. The wireless network uses GPS data from the wireless handset to keep track of the phone's location."

"How does USA Wireless do it?"

Steven replied, "Their method is unique because they use a combination of both techniques. That's why we have had such accurate and reliable location data for the game so far. Like I said before, we use the exact same data the E-911 systems use."

"So you haven't seen a thirty mile error like this?"

"No. I'm not saying there aren't glitches and anomalies, but overall, the LBS data we have seen is accurate. Our problems are more along the lines of accurately translating the LBS data to our GIS, or mapping system, so that the picture we present to the players on their phone maps is accurate."

"So are you saying there is a bug in E-911 or not?"

"Frank, I don't know, let me do some work on it. I can try to get a hold of Larry Hershman at USA Wireless. Jonathan and I just had lunch with him."

"See what you can find out," Frank agreed. "Is it possible that somehow two phones could look the same to the network and that's what caused the location mix up?"

"Are you asking if there was a second phone physically located at the mall that "looked" exactly like Christina's phone to the network? It's not likely. Back in the analog days, that kind of thing happened all the time. That's how people committed cellular fraud. They would steal a phone's identity by capturing the analog signal and then clone a new phone with the same identity. Now with digital wireless networks, all new digital phones are manufactured with a unique identification number, or ESN. The ESN identifies the phone to the network. Since the signal is digital, it is encrypted and cannot be easily stolen. Phone cloning is nearly impossible on advanced, digital wireless networks."

"So how could this happen?"

"I don't know. Let me try to contact Larry. He's the guy we worked with at USA Wireless on the LBS stuff. I can also try to talk to our LBS developer, Patricia Hunter.

She wrote the interface between our game and the USA Wireless LBS server."

"Can you talk to her about this without revealing the investigation?" asked Frank.

"I need to think about how to do that. She is the last person we need knowing about this case."

"Why is that?"

Steven said, "Remember I told you Jonathan had a run in with one of the developers this morning at the game orientation meeting?"

"I'm guessing it was this Patricia Hunter."

"It was. Patricia is our best developer, but she hates Jonathan."

"Why?" Frank's ears perked up.

"Both of them were up for the job of project leader, and I picked Jonathan over her. Patricia thinks the only reason Jonathan was chosen over her was because he's a man, which is totally untrue. She's not happy about getting passed over for the job, so she's been taking it out on Jonathan ever since."

"You think she might have sabotaged the game to make Jonathan look bad?"

"I don't think so. Her code has always performed rock solid. She treats Jonathan like crap, but intentionally writing buggy code would hurt her future career as much as it would hurt Jonathan."

"See what you can find out, but please be discreet. Let's be especially careful with Jonathan and Patricia. Jonathan is definitely a suspect, so we don't want to tip him off to our suspicion. It sounds like Patricia will go public in a heartbeat with any information about the case, especially if it remotely involves Jonathan, just to screw him over. I can't take a chance on details about this case leaking out."

Steven decided not to inform Frank about the supposed fling between Patricia and Larry Hershman that Jonathan had told him about at lunch. Unsure of the validity of the rumor, he opted not to muddy the water without knowing the facts.

They said goodbye, and Frank left Steven's office. Sitting in his chair with his elbows on his desk, Steven cupped his face in his hands and massaged his temples. The error in the E-911 data just did not make sense. The latest game testing showed extremely reliable and accurate location data coming from the LBS server at USA Wireless.

Because of all the distractions of the case, he had not really had a chance to speak in depth with anyone on the team about the results of the previous night's test-game.

Perhaps the game had encountered problems the team had not informed him about yet. They might not have detected that the game had experienced location data problems.

The easiest thing to do would be to call Jonathan and Patricia into the office and dissect the computer logs from last night's game. However, he could not risk tipping either of them off to the murder investigation.

He still doubted that Jonathan killed Christina, but he could not discount the scratches and his potential motive for murdering her. Disobeying Frank and enlisting Jonathan's help in solving the location data mystery was not an option. If Patricia figured out the police considered Jonathan a suspect in a murder case, she would find a way to take Jonathan down, innocent or not.

Damn it! Patricia is no help to me either.

He slapped his desktop.

Steven searched the contacts list on his cell phone for a number, then called Larry Hershman's house. After several rings, the answering machine picked up. If the rumors about Larry and Patricia were true, Larry might be cuddled up with Patricia sleeping off a late night of wild passion. He could be with her at that moment, licking her boots and barking like a dog, or doing whatever the hell those perverts got into. He dialed Larry's cell phone. No answer.

Chapter Eleven

Saturday, November 8 -- 1:44 P.M.

Bobbi sat at a desk in the school newspaper's newsroom. She had contacted every law enforcement agency she could think of in an attempt to get information on the campus crime scene she had found that morning. She had spoken with the city police, the county Sheriff's office and the campus police.

The response from each department's press liaison had been nearly identical: *It is our department's policy to not comment on ongoing investigations. We have no comment at this time.*

She tried every trick she knew of to pull some tidbit of information out of them, but had failed miserably. It was as if whatever she had stumbled onto that morning in the woods behind the softball field had not really existed.

Something big went down in those woods last night, and the cops don't want anyone knowing about it. It must have been a major crime, like a rape or even murder, she thought, basing her theory on the fact that the authorities had prevented her from getting close to the crime scene that morning. *If that damn cop hadn't been so big,* she lamented, *I might have seen something!*

She had, however, observed one crucial detail: Professor Archer had entered the crime scene with a man whom she assumed to be a police detective. She needed to understand Professor Archer's connection to the crime. If she could find and question him, she might have a chance to decipher this mystery and score a front-page scoop.

Bobbi jiggled the mouse, deactivating the screen-saver dancing on the monitor of the PC on the desk in front of her. After logging onto the computer, she pointed the browser to Google and then typed "Steven Archer" into the search field.

Most of the resulting links referenced the university's own website. She did not bother clicking on any of them because she had already read most of this information as part of her initial research for her article on the cell phone game. Continuing to scan the list of hits, she picked a link to an article that profiled the professor's career titled, *Steven Archer: From the Rat Race to the Classroom.* She clicked on the link, which redirected her to the archive section of a website of a popular business and technology magazine.

The article detailed Archer's career, beginning with his first jobs out of college as a software developer. He had quickly made a name for himself by developing several patented internet security software programs. In doing so, he earned the respect of his peers in the software industry and rose quickly to executive management positions.

After successful runs at a few large software companies, Archer left the safety of the Fortune 500 and created his own company specializing in internet security software and consulting. He had timed the market perfectly, and his company's growth exploded as the dot-com era boomed. Just before the bottom dropped out of the technology market, a huge software giant purchased Archer's company, and he retired from the rat race at age thirty-five, a multi-millionaire.

Bobbi continued reading with interest. After less than a year of retirement, Archer apparently grew bored with his life of travel and leisure. As a condition of his company's sale, had he signed a non-compete agreement prohibiting him from creating another security company for a period of seven years. He wanted to start working again so he moved back to his hometown in Florida and pursued a position at the university teaching software development.

Bobbi clicked on a link jumping her to a sidebar profile of Archer. The article portrayed Steven as a thirty-eight year old fun-loving bachelor who enjoyed sports, music and reading. It mentioned that during the school year he split time between his townhouse near campus and his beach house.

Bobbi studied the accompanying picture of Professor Archer. The picture showed a tall, athletic man, dressed in sandals, shorts and a silk Tommy Bahamas shirt, leaning against the rail of a balcony overlooking a beautiful white beach.

This photo must have been taken at the famous beach house, she guessed.

It was definitely the same guy she had seen by the softball field except the light-brown hair, sweaty and matted that morning, was parted on the side and neatly combed in the picture. His tan face featured sparkling blue eyes, the same color as the gentle waves of the Gulf of Mexico visible in the distance behind him. His facial expression, highlighted by a warm, subdued smile, depicted the attitude of a man without a worry on his mind. The man she inspected in the picture did not look as if he would soon enter his forties.

He is totally cute.

The profile said he was single, which ruled out the possibility the cops had called him to the scene because of his wife's involvement in the crime. Perhaps he had a girlfriend that may have been involved. Just because he was single now did not mean he didn't have any children. Was it possible the crime had something to do with a child he had fathered earlier in life?

Bobbi clicked the browser's back button twice to view the page with her original search results. This time she picked a link to an archived newspaper article with the headline, *Internet Guru Helps Nab Killer.*

The story had run in the local paper about six years before. The article told of a killer who had used the internet to meet his victims. The killer had concocted several different scams to find his victims and then lured them into situations where he did unspeakable things to them, always ending in murder.

The authorities asked Archer and his company, considered leaders in internet security, to help solve the case. Archer had personally figured out how the killer anonymously manipulated his victims using internet. He had been responsible for providing the authorities with critical evidence leading to the identification and eventual capture of the heinous murderer.

Archer achieved a bit of fame as he had provided key testimony in the highly publicized Net Stalker trial. Bobbi clicked on an accompanying picture, enlarging it. It showed Professor Archer, dressed in an expensive suit, descending the courthouse steps, flanked by the same detective she had seen him with at the crime scene that morning.

Bobbi smiled as the situation began making sense. She read the caption of the picture.

Star witness, Internet expert Steven Archer, and Detective Frank Diaz leave the courtroom after testifying in the Net Stalker murder trial.

Detective Diaz and Professor Archer had teamed up before to solve a murder case. Were they working together again? Contacting Detective Diaz for information on the case would result in the same canned speech she had heard all day about no commenting on ongoing investigations. No, she decided, locating Professor Archer was her only hope.

Rummaging around the office, she found a faculty directory and looked up Professor Archer's office phone number. She grabbed her desk phone and dialed his number. After punching the final digit, she changed her mind and before the first ring, terminated the call. The professor did not know her.

Why would he talk to me?

The thirty-second phone conversation setting up the interview for her upcoming story had been the only time she had ever spoken to him. She had a zero percent chance of coercing him to speak with her about this case over the phone.

She replaced the office phone receiver in its cradle and grabbed her cell phone. She punched in *67 to avoid transmitting her caller ID information and then dialed the professor's office number.

"This is Professor Archer," answered a voice on the other end of the line. Bobbi quickly clicked off the line, a smile spreading across her face.

I found you!

She logged off the computer, grabbed her stuff and dashed off to the computer center to interview him in person.

Bobbi decided the cops had not called Professor Archer to the crime scene that morning because of a personal relationship he had with someone involved in the crime. The police, specifically Detective Diaz, she guessed, needed his help to solve the crime. He must have called the professor to the crime scene that morning. Apparently, Detective Diaz needed Professor Archer's help again.

Professor Archer utilized his expertise in internet security to help solve the previous murder case, but that had taken place six years before. Would he still be considered an expert in that field today? The terms of the sale of his business prohibited him from working in the internet security field for seven years. Would teaching software development and creating a cell phone game keep his knowledge of internet security current?

Professor Archer had to be involved in the case because of his expertise in software technology. It might be related specifically to cellular or wireless technology, since that seemed to be the basis for his game project. Maybe this crime directly related to his cell phone game. Maybe that was what had upset him when she saw him approach the crime scene that morning.

Bobbi increased her pace realizing the answers to her questions waited in the professor's office just a few hundred yards across campus.

***

Steven sat at his desk, rubbing his eyes. Unable to locate Larry Hershman, he had tried calling all his other contacts at USA Wireless in search of anyone that might help him explain the incorrect E-911 location data. Not a single person on his list had picked up the phone.

Not reaching any of his USA Wireless contacts did not surprise him on such a beautiful fall Saturday on Florida's west coast. Those not outside enjoying the gorgeous weather had probably begun pre-game parties in anticipation of the big college football game scheduled to be televised later that afternoon. Steven wished he were on his balcony at the beach house sipping a cold beer and flipping burgers on the grill with sound of the surf in one ear and pre-game show in the other.

Instead, this case had highjacked his weekend, imprisoning him in his stuffy office with a stomach full of acid and a throbbing headache. He was not about to abandon his mission to explain the thirty-mile error in location data resulting from Christina's 911 call. Solving the LBS anomaly might provide a significant clue to help find her killer. Steven chewed his lower lip, frustrated at not being able to involve Jonathan and Patricia in the investigation. Although enlisting their help would make his task easier, Steven refused to defy Frank's strict orders to leave them out.

Steven remembered when he and Frank first met while working on the famous Net Stalker murders. Little initial evidence had existed in that case and they faced searching the entire cyber world for the killer. They had pursued the proverbial needle in the internet haystack.

Still very much in its infancy then, the untamed internet provided a digital Wild West for its users. Their suspect had been an outlaw in a cyber world with few laws. But he and Frank made a good team, and they had eventually corralled their man.

Steven shook his head, realizing this case, less than six hours old, had already created more difficulty and caused more pain for him than the entire Net Stalker case, which had lasted weeks. The last time, he had chased a faceless murderer with victims unknown to him. This case affected him personally, as the victim and the prime suspect turned out to be close friends. His project and his future at the university were quite possibly at stake.

Steven heard a knock on the door, and Peter Vaughn sauntered into his office.

"You don't look so good. Are you okay, Professor Archer?"

"I'm fine. I've just got a lot on my mind at the moment."

"Did you hear what happened with Jonathan and Patricia at the orientation meeting this morning?"

"I did, I spoke to Jonathan at lunch."

"I thought Jonathan was going to kill Patricia. She sure knows how to piss him off."

"Yeah, she can get a little, well you know—"

"You should've seen the look on Jonathan's face. I mean, he had veins popping out on his forehead and neck. His face was bright red. I thought I was going to have to hold him back from jumping on her."

"I'm sure that Jonathan would never—"

"Patricia was eating it up. She was giving Jonathan a look that just dared him to do something. You know she's just trying to get him in trouble so she can get his job."

"Those two are under a lot of pressure. They've both got a lot riding on this project. We're in the final stages of this thing, and they're stressed out, that's all."

"If you say so. I think they hate each other. Patricia would do just about anything to get rid of Jonathan and take his job. If she could somehow get rid of him and you promoted her to project leader...that would be huge. Jeez, who wouldn't want to get in line for a big time gig at USA Wireless?"

"I don't think—"

"You know Patricia is screwing Larry Hershman, right?"

Am I the only person on the planet that didn't know this bit of gossip?

Before Steven could respond, Peter continued. "I hear Hershman's pretty upset that his company is planning to pass him over and hire Jonathan for the job. That's a real kick in the teeth. I'll betcha Patricia's throwing gasoline on that fire every chance she gets."

"Peter, listen, can you do me a favor and not talk about what happened between Jonathan and Patricia this morning? We are so close to the end of this thing, I just can't afford to have this project blow up, understand?"

"Sure, Professor Archer, I won't say a thing. By the way, I've been asking Jonathan about getting more involved with the game development, you know, what we talked about before, and he still won't discuss it with me."

"Peter, I know you want to be on the development team, but like I told you before, it's Jonathan's decision as project leader, not mine."

Peter's jaw tightened, and his expression grew angry. Head down, he turned and ambled to the door to leave. "Pete, wait. Listen, I can't promise you anything, but I'll talk to Jonathan about it, okay?"

"Jeez, that's just great, thanks." He offered Steven a grateful smile. "And you can count on me to keep my mouth shut about Jonathan and Patricia." He turned again to leave.

"Thanks. Hey, one more thing. You've been monitoring the results of the test-games pretty closely, right?" Steven asked.

"Sure, why?" Peter answered with a shrug.

"How accurate has the LBS location data from USA Wireless been lately?"

"Pinpoint, right on the money," Peter replied.

"Nothing's changed, we still use the same data feed and LBS server from USA Wireless?"

"Yeah."

Steven chewed his bottom lip then asked, "It's still the same data they use for E-911, right?"

"Sure, you know that." Peter arched a brow, "Why? What's up?"

Steven shook his head, "It's just...never mind."

Be careful what you say.

120

"I'm just curious if anything with the LBS data feed has changed recently, that's all. Did you look at the results of last night's test-game?"

"Not yet," Peter replied. "I've been too busy today. I had a server go down last night. It's just a test server, not production, thank God. I wanted to make sure it's ready for next week so I've been rebuilding it today, sorry."

"No problem. One last thing, do we still have access to the LBS server at USA Wireless?"

"If you mean can we log onto their server, sure, just in case we need to tweak the LBS data interface."

"Do you know who on our team has access to that LBS server?"

"Patricia has an account since she wrote the interface code. I think Jonathan has access as well, although I really don't know why he would have any reason to log onto the LBS server. It's not like he wrote that code, you know?"

"Okay, thanks. And thanks again for keeping the Jonathan and Patricia thing quiet."

"No problem." Smiling, Peter left Steven's office.

***

Steven stood and stretched. The office desk clock read two-thirty in the afternoon, and his body ached. He felt like he could crawl into his bed and sleep for two straight days. In a daze, he rambled down the stairs to the lobby on the first floor of the computer center and bought a *Diet Pepsi* from a vending machine.

Popping open the can, Steven contemplated the E-911 location data mystery. Why had the E-911 location data from Christina's 911 call been off by thirty miles? The game tests to date had shown extremely accurate location data, and the game software utilized the exact same location data generated by USA Wireless that fed the county's E-911 system.

The discrepancy did not make sense because the USA Wireless network used a combination of triangulation and GPS data to ensure pinpoint accuracy of the LBS data. A combination of the two different methods determined the location of the cell phone. The software compared the results of each method, and if the two locations differed by more than a predetermined error factor, then the program reported an exception error and threw out the bad location.

The system achieved a second level of accountability when the program checked the current location of the cellular handset, reported against the previously reported location. Humans can move on the earth only so fast, so the computer compared the two locations. If the program calculated an impossibly large delta between the previous location and the current location, meaning a person could not have possibly traveled that distance in that amount of time, then the system reported an exception error and did not use the data.

The location data for Christina's 911 call broke *both* of the error checks and yet the system still had sent the erroneous data from the LBS server at USA Wireless to the PSAP. Could this have happened coincidentally on a murder victim's phone just prior to her being killed?

"That would be one hell of a coincidental bug," Steven mumbled.

No, someone or something had somehow manipulated the LBS location data.

Acid churned in Steven's stomach, and he needed some air. He walked from the vending machines through the lobby doors and into the bright sunshine. Steven concluded someone must have hacked the LBS server at USA Wireless causing the E-911 data error.

If he could find the person who had hacked the LBS server, he would learn the identity of Christina's killer. Only a few people could access that server who also had the ability to hack the software, namely, Larry Hershman at USA Wireless, and Jonathan and Patricia from the university. Steven just couldn't believe Jonathan would be involved.

No mental slouch, Patricia had the brains to frame Jonathan. Would she set him up just to get his job? Patricia knew more about LBS than anyone on the team, including Jonathan. She wrote the LBS interface code for the game project. She had access to the LBS servers and certainly possessed the skill needed to hack the software.

Larry Hershman from USA Wireless also possessed an in-depth knowledge of the LBS system. He worked closely with Patricia on the development of the LBS interface for the WILCO Project game. Larry had recently suffered setbacks in both his personal life and his career. His wife unexpectedly ran out on him during the Christmas holiday the previous year. As a result, he began drinking too much and his job performance suffered. Jonathan's stock on the project skyrocketed while Larry's plummeted. As a result, Larry had all but lost his promotion to Director at USA Wireless to Jonathan.

Steven scratched the light stubble on his chin. Larry might have additional reasons for wanting to force Jonathan out of the picture. He needed the extra income the promotion to a Director level would provide. He admitted to Steven that his second wife had taken him to the cleaners in their recent divorce, and he was broke. Although USA Wireless had not officially awarded Jonathan the job of Director yet, the gossip around the office had already humiliated Larry. The water cooler chatter at USA Wireless had the industry veteran passed over for the big promotion, defeated by a young kid with no professional experience.

Was that sufficient motive for Larry to kill Christina and frame Jonathan for the crime? Steven drew several deep breaths and plodded back up the stairs to his office without the usual spring in his step. He needed to focus and analyze all the scenarios. Despite the many factors pointing to Jonathan, none of them *proved* he killed Christina. The LBS system at USA Wireless might not have been hacked.

He reminded himself that regardless of the power and sophistication of modern computers, they accomplished nothing by themselves and needed programming by humans. Humans invariably made mistakes. The incorrect E-911 location data, although unlikely, could have been the result of an innocent programming error, a simple bug in the system. Steven needed to determine who had accessed the LBS server at

USA Wireless and if the LBS software had been manipulated.

Chapter Twelve

Saturday, November 8 -- 2:44 P.M.

Bobbi Cline peered through Professor Archer's open office door in the computer center. He sat behind his desk with his back to her, gazing out the windows that made up the entire back wall of the office. With the professor unaware of her presence, Bobbi surveyed the tidy room, surprised at how orderly it appeared compared to the faculty offices she frequented. Most of the offices in the English and journalism departments seemed gloomy in comparison with dusty stacks of newspapers and periodicals and endless piles of books heaped everywhere.

The room appeared more like a corporate office than that of an academic professor. Sunlight streamed through the large windows, and fluorescent light from the overhead fixture reflected off the white walls, brightly illuminating the room. An L-shaped computer desk consumed half of the space. Above the desk to her left hung a large, framed poster featuring an aerial view of the university football stadium filled with colorfully dressed fans on game day.

Eager to check out the rest of the office, Bobbi inched through the doorframe. Dozens of neatly framed diplomas, certificates, plaques, and awards covered the right wall. The bio she had read on the internet that morning had not done Professor Archer's career justice. Several framed pictures of a slightly younger version of the professor, dressed in dark suits or tuxedos, accepting various awards hung on the wall amid the other items. Steven Archer had been a regular celebrity nerd before he had cashed out and retired, she concluded.

Bobbi cleared her throat and said, "Excuse me, Professor Archer?"

He flinched at the sound of her voice and spinning his chair around to face her, replied, "Yes, can I help you?"

He had aged well and looked as handsome to her in person as he did in the picture she had seen earlier on the Web, but his face bore a weary, tired expression. Missing now was his attractive smile and the sparkle in his eyes she had admired.

"I'm Bobbi Cline. We spoke last week about your cell phone game." He offered her a quizzical look. "I'm doing an article for the school paper, and we had scheduled an interview."

Professor Archer spun his chair around and snatched his cell phone that sat charging next to his PC. Without stopping, he completed the full spin and faced Bobbi again. Staring at the screen, he thumbed a couple of buttons. "I thought we were scheduled for next—"

"We are, but I need to talk to you now. It can't wait until next week."

"I'm sorry, but right now is not a good time. You're going to have to wait for our appointment."

"This can't wait until next week."

"I know, you've got a deadline and you need some extra time. Look, I don't mean to be rude, but I just do not have time to talk to you now. I'll see you next week."

Professor Archer whirled his chair back around and started typing on his keyboard. She turned to go and then stopped.

Damn it!

She refused to leave the office without getting some information about the crime scene. Her only hope for keeping the most important story of her career alive sat at the desk behind her.

She flipped back around to face Professor Archer and opened her mouth to ask him if he knew anything about a crime committed on campus the previous night.

Wait, she smiled, *there is a better way to do this.*

"I'm sorry, Professor Archer?"

He spun back around and faced her with an expression that did not portray anger as much as tired frustration. With a stern tone he interrupted, "I've told you for the final time, I can't talk to you right now. If you don't leave my office immediately, I'm calling campus security and you can forget about our interview next week, understand?"

Taking a deep breath, Bobbi stared directly into his gaze. "I know about the murder on campus last night," she lied. "I know you're involved."

Professor Archer's mouth dropped open. His eyes narrowed, and he tilted his head slightly.

"How do you—please, shut the door and have a seat."

Heart racing, Bobbi pulled the door closed and sat in one of the chairs facing his desk.

"I saw you this morning at the crime scene with Detective Frank Diaz."

"Do the police know that you know about the murder?"

"The police stopped me when I was investigating the crime scene."

"Investigating the crime scene? How did you find out about it?"

Bobbi's first reaction was to ignore the question so as not to give away how little she knew about the situation.

No, time to play it straight, she reasoned.

Another lie would eventually backfire, Professor Archer would lose trust in her, and she desperately needed him on her side.

"I stumbled across the crime scene while walking across campus this morning."

"And the police told you about the murder?"

"Well...um, not exactly."

"If they didn't tell you then you tricked me." An angry frown formed on his face. "You didn't even know there was a murder until I told you, right?"

Bobbi offered him a sheepish smile that stated, *Don't hate me because I'm good.*

"Yeah, I guess so, sorry about that. See, I knew something big went down in the woods because of the crime scene tape and how the cops treated me when I walked up."

She told him how they had forced her back from the scene and then later enlarged the perimeter because she had managed to venture too close.

"So how did you see me if you were so far away?"

"I saw you when you first got there, before you went into the woods. You seemed very upset. I couldn't tell what you and the detective were arguing about, but I heard you yell. Then he calmed you down, and you guys walked toward the crime scene in the woods."

Professor Archer shook his head, staring off in the distance, almost trance-like.

"Why were you there, at the crime scene, this morning?" she asked, bringing his focus back to her.

"I really can't talk to you about this."

"Who is the victim? Did you know the victim?" Bobbi pressed.

"Please, I can't talk to you," he insisted.

"Did Detective Diaz call you to the crime scene to get your help on the case?"

Professor Archer's eyes widened slightly.

That's it!

Without saying a word, Professor Archer just confirmed her theory that Detective Diaz asked him to help on the case. "I know you two teamed up on the Net Stalker case years ago," she said, pushing harder.

"You remember that? You must have been in junior high school back then."

"Yeah, I was just a kid, but I've done some research on you." She flashed him a smile. "I'm a reporter. I get the story, that's what I do. And I'm going to get this one, so how about giving me a hand?"

"I'd really like to help you out, but thanks to your trick, I've already said too much," Steven said firmly and whirled back facing his PC. "Good luck with your story, and if you still want to meet next week to talk about the game, I'll see you then."

Bobbi dropped her card on the desk, said goodbye, and, with a huge grin on her face, left the office.

She had taken a huge risk when she lied to Professor Archer, but the gamble had paid off. Having no choice, Bobbi tricked him into revealing the murder. She did not feel the slightest guilt for using deception because her job entailed uncovering the truth and reporting it at any cost.

Beyond confirming the crime scene had actually been the site of a murder investigation, she had failed to extract further detailed information from Professor Archer about the case. He had not verbally confirmed Detective Diaz had enlisted his help to solve the crime, but his subtle change of expression had betrayed to her that he had asked the professor to work with him.

If this situation paralleled the Net Stalker case, then Detective Diaz needed help with some technological aspect. Bobbi narrowed the scenarios down to three possibilities. First, the case might involve internet security, Professor Archer's former field of expertise. Second, software development, his current forte, played a role in the investigation. Or lastly, the case had something to do with wireless technology, which related to his current game project.

Regarding possibility number one, Bobbi guessed Professor Archer probably still knew more on internet security than almost anyone in the field did. Could this case involve the internet like the Net Stalker case? If not for his knowledge of internet security, would Detective Diaz have drafted the professor for his expertise in software development?

Duh, software doesn't kill people, Bobbi concluded, swatting herself in the forehead.

She could not find any link between developing software and the campus murder. On the other hand, wireless technology could definitely be involved in this murder case. Especially since the game seemed to utilize many advanced wireless features.

The cops had either involved Professor Archer because of his expertise in the internet or advanced wireless technology. She did not expect to receive any further cooperation from him on this case as the cops had obviously told him to keep quiet. She winced, realizing she might have slammed the door on him as a further source of information by using deceit and trickery to garner information.

Time to step up to the plate and play hardball. Her next move would be to speak with Detective Diaz. A frown formed on her face as she pondered how she might persuade him to talk.

This is not gonna be easy.

Chapter Thirteen

Saturday, November 8 -- 2:52 P.M.

As soon as Bobbi Cline disappeared from his office doorway, Steven realized a smart young woman had duped him. He shook his head in disbelief, asking himself how he could have fallen for the cub reporter's trick. Frank would be pissed when he found out some pesky kid had stumbled on the crime scene that morning. Not just any kid as it turned out, but a bright, gutsy, tenacious kid, who just so happened to write for the school newspaper.

Steven grabbed the phone and dialed Frank's office. He did not pick up, so Steven tried his cell phone. No answer, so he left a message detailing his conversation with Bobbi.

Sucking in a deep breath, Steven drummed his fingers on the desktop and contemplated his next move. Scanning the office, his gazed fixed on a gold-framed picture of his niece, posing in her high school graduation gown, mortarboard perched on her head, proudly clutching her newly earned diploma. When the realization that a female student, just like Jenny, had been brutally murdered the previous night hit, his body shuddered as a wave of fear for his niece's safety washed over him.

Steven snatched the phone and dialed Jenny's dorm room, but she did not answer. He hung up and punched in the number to her cell phone. Two rings—she did not pick up. She was probably at a pre-game party with friends. Two more rings—she still did not answer.

Damn it, Jenny, please pick up!

Another ring and then her voice came on the line.

"Hi, it's Jenny. Leave your number, and I just might call you back."

He listened to the same sweet voice he had heard on her voicemail that morning as he sprinted to the crime scene. The shocking images of Christina's sheet-covered body and lifeless face flooded back into his mind. Christina's killer still prowled the campus. Panic grabbed at his gut again. Trying to sound calm, he left a message for her to call him as soon as she got the message.

Steven stared out of his office window. Now was not the time to lose focus. He desperately needed to figure out why the location data from Christina's 911 call had been incorrect. He scratched his chin, trying to remain calm. So far, his efforts to reach Larry Hershman, his contact at USA Wireless, had been unsuccessful. Hesitant to disobey Frank's edict not to divulge the investigation to Jonathan or Patricia, he felt helpless.

"Fuck it," he growled under his breath. Grabbing the receiver from the cradle for a third time, he dialed Jonathan's office extension. The phone rang several times and then his voicemail picked up. Before Jonathan's outgoing message completed, Steven slammed the receiver back on the cradle. Chewing his lip, he snatched the receiver and dialed Patricia's office extension. No answer.

Steven flew out of his chair and raced across the floor to Jonathan's office. To his disappointment, he found the door closed. Even though Jonathan had not answered his office phone, he still might be working in there. Steven carefully placed his ear to the door, but did not hear a sound. He knocked firmly on the closed door for several seconds then waited. No response. Jonathan was not there.

Shaking his head, he sprinted to Patricia's cubicle, which he found vacant as well. He double-timed his way around the remaining offices and cubicles, checking to see if anyone else on the development team happened to be working and found the entire area empty.

Mumbling obscenities under his breath, he moved down the hall to the far end of the floor and peered through the plate glass window into the secured computer room. Steven smiled.

Finally, he thought, *someone I can always count on.*

Steven banged on the thick glass window. After a few seconds, Peter looked toward him. Pointing back down the hall, Steven mouthed, "My office." Peter nodded and gave him the okay sign.

Steven hustled back to his office, and a few moments later the system administrator rumbled through the doorway.

"What's up?"

"Have you seen Jonathan or Patricia around today?"

"I saw them both this morning in the auditorium, but I haven't seen Patricia in the office today. Jonathan was here earlier, but he left a little while ago."

"Okay, thanks. Peter, can I trust you?"

"Oh, sure, I promise I won't talk about that argument Jonathan and Patricia had this morning."

"Good. But there's something else I need your help with, and I really need you to keep it between us. You can't tell anyone."

Peter's eyes grew wide, and he slowly nodded his head.

"Of course. Jeez, you can trust me, Professor Archer."

"Good. I really appreciate it, Peter."

"No sweat. So what do you need?"

Steven took a deep breath. "I need you to help me find out who has logged into the LBS server at the USA Wireless data center in the past month or so. Can you help me with that?"

"Sure."

Steven exhaled, relieved. This helped solve his problem without having to involve Jonathan or Patricia. "Great! How long will it take you to get the information?"

"I can show you right now if you want."

"Perfect, that would be very helpful."

Peter walked behind Steven's desk and sat at his PC. He clicked open a terminal emulation window and began typing a string of commands in rapid succession.

"First, let's jump onto the LBS data comm server on the production LAN." While his fingers darted across the keyboard, he gave a running commentary on the steps he executed. Steven was not sure if Peter made his comments for his benefit or if he was just thinking aloud.

"Okay, now we telnet to the LBS server at the USA Wireless data center. Got it."

Peter had connected to the LBS server through a dedicated T1 line from the university to the USA Wireless data center. This private communication channel provided completely secure data communication between the two sites at lightning fast speeds.

A message displayed on the screen saying "Property of USA Wireless Inc. Restricted Server. Unauthorized Access Prohibited," and after entering his ID and password, Peter had logged into the LBS server at USA Wireless.

Peter typed in a command Steven recognized as one giving him "root" or "super user" account privileges on the server. In order to gain the all powerful "root" privileges, Peter had exploited a little known security hole in the UNIX operating system that the system administrators at USA Wireless should have patched but had not, leaving the system wide open for a hacker like Peter. Normally Steven would have been upset at the lax security on the corporate server, but in this situation, he felt lucky and thankful the vulnerability existed and Peter had been smart enough to utilize it to help him retrieve the information he desperately needed.

"Okay, let's look at logins for the past thirty days," Peter said, typing in a cryptic looking command that produced several columns of data, including user names with corresponding dates and times of login sessions. They paged through a couple of screens of data. "There's Hershman's ID. It looks like there are only three logins from the university. See how all the university user names have the same suffix? I'm going to issue the same command and "grep" for just the university logins."

Peter hit a control sequence on the keyboard bringing up the same command, added a few characters to the end of the command and hit the return key. The same columns of data returned to the screen, but the output showed only the login records for the three university login ID's.

"Who do the three logins belong to?" Steven asked.

"One of them is me, and the other two are Jonathan and Patricia."

"No one else from the development team or the university has logged into that server?"

"Nope. Take a look. There is a single entry for me. It's time stamped just about a minute ago. That's the record for the session we're using right now. Patricia has a dozen or so logins, which makes sense since she wrote the interface to the LBS data feed. But look here, over the past week or so it looks like Jonathan has been nosing around on the server as well."

"It looks like he has been on the server a handful of times. When was the last time he logged on?"

"Looks like just yesterday. I still can't understand why Jonathan has all of a sudden been jumping onto the LBS server."

"Okay, that's what I needed to know. Go ahead and log out."

Fingers flying across the keyboard, Peter logged off all of the servers they had accessed.

"What's going on, Professor Archer? Is there a problem with the LBS data or something?"

"No, I don't think so."

"So why do you want to know who's been getting on the LBS server? You think Jonathan's been screwing with Patricia's code?"

"No."

"Wanna know what I think? I'll betcha Jonathan is scared that Patricia is sabotaging the game so he's checking up on her code and stuff." Peter closed the terminal emulation window, stood and faced Steven.

"Peter, remember our agreement. I'm trusting you to keep this between us, okay?"

"You got it. I won't tell a soul."

"Thanks."

Peter left the office and lumbered back down the hall toward the computer room.

Chapter Fourteen

Saturday, November 8 -- 3:37 P.M.

As soon as Peter left his office and disappeared from sight down the hall, Steven collapsed into his chair. Jonathan had spent time on the LBS server in the past few weeks and had logged on as recently as yesterday, the day before Christina's murder.

Steven had hoped to find Jonathan had not accessed the LBS server recently. If he had not logged onto the server at USA Wireless then it would have been impossible for him to hack the LBS software and thus manipulate the E-911 data. But Steven had seen the report with his own eyes, Jonathan had logged on the LBS server at least six times over the past week. That, however, did not mean Jonathan had hacked the LBS software to manipulate the location data; it just meant he had the opportunity to do so.

Observing that Patricia had logged into the LBS server multiple times did not surprise him, although to his knowledge, the LBS interface code she had developed had not changed in the past month. She could have made minor changes to her interface code and had just not reported them.

Steven shook his head, reached for his notebook. He divided a blank page into three columns and then labeled each column with a set of initials: JH, PH and LH. Below the initials, on the left side of the page he scrawled, "Access LBS—why?"

What had been Jonathan's purpose for accessing the LBS server? Under the initials JH, Steven jotted, "Check PH's code?" Maybe Peter's theory was right—Jonathan had merely been doing his job and checking up on Patricia's work. If that were the case, then why had they not seen problems in the location data during the game tests? The WILCO Project game used the exact same location data that the E-911 system used. Her interface code had been working great and the location data coming from the LBS servers had been pinpoint accurate—until last night. Jonathan would have had no reason to check Patricia's code unless he suspected that she planned to sabotage the game.

Steven added a comment in the LH column, "PH sabotage game?" Maybe Jonathan knew she was up to something and had begun building a case against her. Why wouldn't Jonathan have come to him about his suspicions? Maybe he did not want to say anything because he had not yet gathered the proper evidence to prove his case against her. Had he been anticipating a situation like the previous night where someone had manipulated the location data, and did he suspect Patricia to be the manipulator?

Steven rubbed his eyes and then under the PH heading, he wrote, "Changed location data?" Was it possible that Patricia had manipulated the LBS location data? If so, did that mean she had masterminded the murder? Why would she want to kill Christina?

He added a note, "Frame JH—why?" Perhaps her motive was to frame Jonathan so she could slide into his position and eventually steal the job at USA Wireless. The position would be worth hundreds of thousands of dollars, millions, potentially with the stock options. On the other hand, was she so outraged that he'd picked a good-looking male over an equally capable female for the project manager position that she decided to punish Jonathan?

Steven's focus shifted to Larry Hershman, who also had accessed the LBS server frequently over the past month. Under LH he scratched, "Working with PH— legit?" He certainly could have been working with Patricia to make minor adjustments to her LBS interface programs.

147

Then Steven scribbled, "Non-game work?" as Larry could also have just been doing work unrelated to the WILCO Project on the LBS server for USA Wireless.

In the same column, Steven wrote, "JH revenge?" Larry had as much motive as Patricia to see Jonathan go down in flames. Had Larry set up Jonathan to remove him from the picture so he could redeem himself professionally and claim the promotion he believed he rightfully deserved?

Staring at his chicken-scratch, Steven concluded that his theories seemed far-fetched, especially when compared to the straightforward evidence against Jonathan. Steven counted on his fingers as he reeled off the points against Jonathan. One, a nasty split with his fiancée, two, telltale facial scratches, three, his admitted presence in the woods the night of the murder, and now four, the proof that he had spent time working on the LBS server, giving him the opportunity to hack the LBS software and perhaps manipulate the E-911 location data. Steven frowned. Although the evidence appeared circumstantial, it did not paint a positive picture for Jonathan.

Over the years, Steven and Jonathan's relationship had evolved. He recalled that they had first met when

Jonathan took several of his programming classes as an undergrad. He shook his head.

That seems like ages ago.

Now, with Jonathan currently enrolled in the post-graduate program and working as the project manager for the WILCO Project, Steven had become his mentor and boss. This transition had allowed them to build a closer personal relationship, and they had become good friends.

Jonathan portrayed many of Steven's traits. Smart and driven, they both shared a passion for computers and technology. However, Steven had also noticed a dark side to Jonathan. He looked down on those he perceived not of his ilk. Steven considered him a snob and attributed this attitude and behavior to his upbringing.

When Steven had first met Jonathan, he had been cocky and egotistical. He had reminded him of Hollywood's version of the popular-but-shallow frat boy. Steven respected his academic prowess, but did not care for his personality.

He's a different person now.

Over the past year-and-a-half, Jonathan's attitude had matured. He had become less snobbish and more tolerant of others. Steven hoped Jonathan's positive change in behavior had been at least partially due to his mentoring.

He had worked hard to soften Jonathan's snobby attitude and while he had improved, he still had a long way to go.

Steven had grown to like the new Jonathan and he wanted him to succeed, but Jonathan was far from perfect. He still had a tendency to fall back, but he also made an honest effort to change for the better.

Jonathan is certainly no murderer, he concluded.

Steven picked up the phone and dialed Jonathan's apartment. The phone rang several times, and an answering machine picked up. Steven left a message for Jonathan to call him as soon possible. Unable to reach him on his cell phone, he left the same urgent message.

***

Bobbi Cline sat in a chair in the deserted Laundromat, reading the Saturday newspaper. The afternoon football game had apparently made her one of the few students left on campus not guzzling beer in front of a TV. Despite the peace and quiet of the normally packed room, she found herself unable to concentrate on the day's news. She typically devoured the newspaper each day, reading every word of every story in the national, metro and commentary sections as well as most, if not all, of the feature stories. This afternoon she could not get through a single article without her mind drifting to the murder case.

Her cell phone rang. She had a hunch the caller might be Detective Diaz. Bobbi smiled, knowing the message she left earlier on Detective Diaz's voicemail would get his attention. Her message had been simple:

This is Bobbi Cline, I am a reporter, and I know about the murder in the woods on campus last night. Call me.

She'd concluded her message by giving him her cell phone number slowly and clearly, repeating it twice. Bobbi answered her phone.

"Hello."

"Is this Bobbi Cline?"

"Yes, this is Bobbi."

"Ms. Cline, this is Detective Frank Diaz returning your call."

Bobbi's stomach filled with butterflies. This was her chance to break the biggest story of her career. She nervously yanked the small spiral notebook from the back pocket of her jeans.

"Thanks for calling me back, Detective. I just need to ask you a few questions about the murder that occurred on campus last night."

"Do I know you, Ms. Cline?"

"We've never met."

"You mentioned on your message that you are a reporter. Who do you work for?"

"I'm on the staff of the campus newspaper."

"Great," Detective Diaz mumbled. "Just why do you believe there was a murder on campus?"

Bobbi's stomach did a flip. This would be her one and only opportunity to get this story.

I can't screw this up!

A drop of sweat trickled from her underarm down her side. She summoned her courage and pushed on.

"Are you denying that you are investigating a murder?"

"I've had just about enough of this bullshit," Detective Diaz answered in a stern tone. "I don't have time for games right now, young lady. Where did you hear about a murder case?"

Anticipating the tough cop act, Bobbi sucked in a deep breath. "I know you think I'm just some kid working on the student newspaper, but I'm a real reporter and people do read our paper. I also know lots of reporters from the city paper and the TV stations. I'm just trying to find out the real story on what happened in the woods last night. If you don't want to tell me what's going on, then be prepared for breaking news during the football game about a body found in the woods on campus this morning."

The phone grew silent for several seconds. Bobbi coughed uncomfortably, unsure if the threat had worked or if he had hung up. He finally responded, "Okay, let's just take it easy here. No one needs to go to the TV guys, all right?"

Bobbi tried unsuccessfully to stifle a sigh of relief—she remained in the game. Detective Diaz did not seem like the type that appreciated threats.

Best not to push my luck here.

"Fine. Are you going to tell me what's going on or should I ask you?"

"Here are the ground rules," the detective interrupted sharply. "You don't say anything to anybody or write a single sentence about this case until I tell you, understand?"

"Yeah, but—"

"No buts or we don't have a deal. Believe me, this is not an ideal situation for me, but the reality is I am going to have to trust you, and you are going to have to trust me, okay?"

"Okay."

"So, I will tell you what I can about the case and let you know when it is okay to write about it. You cannot talk to anyone about this case or our arrangement. Not your boyfriend, not your mother, not your priest, no one! You get one chance, Ms. Cline. You slip up one single time, and you might as well get ready to write movie reviews and gardening columns for the rest of your career, because you will *never* get cooperation from me or any other police department around here ever again. I'll see to it, you understand?"

"Blackballed," Bobbi mumbled under her breath. She cleared her throat and answered, "Yeah, I got it."

"Good. One more thing, don't ever threaten me like that again."

"Yes sir." Bobbi swallowed hard and croaked, "About the mur—"

"Stop! Rule number two. Never speak about the details of this case over the phone. You might think I'm being paranoid, but it's crucial that details about the incident in the woods last night are kept strictly confidential at this point in the investigation."

Rings of sweat grew on her shirt beneath her underarms, and her hands trembled from a combination of fear and excitement. "Sorry."

"The incident in the woods *is* what you think it is." Detective Diaz had made his point, and his voice became less abrasive. "My question to you is, how did you figure it out? Professor Archer told me you saw us near the woods this morning."

"I just happened to walk past all the activity and I recognized the, uh scene, you know, with the tape and all. I figured there must be something pretty serious going on back in the woods."

"So you're the reason Sergeant Bryant had to move his perimeter back," said Diaz. "Did you tell him that you are a reporter?"

"Yeah, and he moved me all the way back behind the backstop of the softball field. He wouldn't tell me a thing."

"He better not have. He told me someone had gotten too close to the scene, but he neglected to tell me it was a reporter. So when you talked to Professor Archer you really had no idea what was going on? Did you just make an educated guess?"

"That's right. I told him I had seen the two of you near the woods. I asked him why he was there, but he wouldn't tell me anything. He was about to throw me out of his office. I was desperate, so I tricked him by saying I knew about the, you know, incident, and that he was involved."

"That's pretty damn sneaky. Not bad for a college kid," Diaz conceded.

"Thanks." Exhaling, Bobbi relaxed a little. "So am I the only press, um, aware of the incident?"

"As far as we know, yes."

"How have you kept this thing such a big secret?"

"It's been pure luck. The roommates of the affected are out of town for the weekend. The family has been unbelievably cooperative. They understand the need to keep this thing quiet to give us a better chance of finding whoever is responsible for this incident. The maintenance crew that discovered the situation has also fully cooperated. Everyone has managed to keep their mouths shut so far, but we don't know how long this can last. It's a miracle that other than you, the scene was not discovered by anyone else. Hopefully, our luck will continue until we can break this case. Ms. Cline, I've got to go. No story yet. Remember what I said, not a word to anyone. I'll be in touch."

Bobbi jumped out of the chair after Diaz disconnected. She pumped her fist and let out a satisfying yell, "Yes!" A drop of sweat flew off her arm, and she noticed that her sweat-soaked shirt clung to her torso. She bounded over to the dryer and yanked out a warm, nearly dry towel and wiped off her face, neck and arms.

If she could trust Detective Diaz, and she had no reason not to, she was going to be writing the biggest front-page story the school newspaper had ever printed. This could be the break she had been looking for, the big story that would launch her career. The city paper would run a front-page article on the murder, giving the campus newspaper credit for breaking the story first. The wire services might even pick it up. Because of her article, this case could become national news and she would elevate herself to the ace reporter on the campus newspaper staff. Those clippings in her portfolio would be the ones that would get her interviews with the big boys after graduation.

Feeling light-headed and overwhelmed, she fell back down in the chair. There really had been a murder committed in those woods last night. Despite the stuffy heat in the laundry room, a chill enveloped her damp body. Someone brutally murdered a fellow student on campus and she had landed right smack in the middle of the case. A slight feeling of nausea passed through her and exhaustion overtook her body.

Be careful what you ask for, because you just might get it.

Chapter Fifteen

Saturday, November 8 -- 3:51 P.M.

Steven sat at his office desk, his stomach rumbling loudly. The clock read three fifty-one in the afternoon, and the only thing he had eaten that day had been a protein bar. The two hundred and twenty calories he consumed early that morning had long since burned off. His body needed food, but his mind rebelled at the thought of eating.

Steven's office phone rang. Knots of stress replaced the hunger pangs in his stomach. Part of him hoped Jonathan had finally decided to return his call. He would have liked nothing better than to confront him with the situation and then have Jonathan respond with a credible alibi, proving he could not possibly be the killer.

He should have listened to Frank's demand to resist contacting Jonathan about the case. Having now convinced himself that Jonathan must be on the other end of the phone, Steven panicked. What was he going to tell

Jonathan when he asked why Steven had called? Steven's heart raced. His mind froze. He considered letting the call go to voicemail, but at the last second picked up the receiver.

"This is Steven."

"Uncle Steven, its Jenny. You've called me twice in one day, what a treat. What's up?"

"Hi, Jenny." Steven blew out a huge breath of air. "Thanks for calling back. Are you okay?"

"Yeah. Everything is great. Sorry I didn't call you back sooner. A group of us girls went on a canoeing trip down the river. We just got back."

"No problem. Hey, what do you and your friends have going on tonight? Any special plans?"

"Not really. We're all pretty beat from the canoeing trip. We were just going to rent some DVD's and chill."

"Do you think you and your friends would be interested in hanging out at my beach place tonight? I'll cook dinner, and you and the girls can stay over and hang at the beach tomorrow."

"Sounds cool to me. They are right here, let me ask them, hold on."

Steven expected them to turn his offer down. No matter how young and cool he still felt, teenagers thought adults in their late thirties were decidedly uncool, especially those who taught at their college.

Dear God, please let them say yes, he prayed.

"Uncle Steven, sounds great. We'd love to come to the beach."

Steven exhaled with relief. "Fantastic. Dinner will be ready at six-thirty. Invite as many girls as you want."

Jenny thanked him and they hung up. Smiling, Steven closed his eyes and inhaled deeply. He tilted his head back and exhaled slowly, feeling the tension drain from his neck and shoulders.

Opening his eyes, Steven sat straight. He had cleverly managed to convince his niece and her friends to stay an hour away from campus at his beach house and had pulled it off without having to go against Frank's edict forbidding him to reveal anything about the case. He chuckled aloud. He felt almost as crafty as the student reporter who had tricked him into revealing the murder earlier.

Having the girls stay at the beach did not guarantee their safety, but the house did have a monitored security system and was located some sixty miles from the site of the murder. In addition, because the beach drew so many tourists, the cops patrolled the area around the house and property constantly. Needing to insure they would not venture back to the campus, Steven vowed not to let his niece and her friends out of his sight that night.

***

Later that afternoon, Steven packed up his laptop computer to head for the beach house. He needed to buy the food and prepare dinner for Jenny and her friends. Although a killer remained at large, and he had made little progress in solving the E-911 location data mystery, a huge smile stretched across his face. At least Jenny would be safely away from campus, staying at the beach house under his watchful eye.

Slinging his laptop case strap across his shoulder, Steven walked to the office door. He had a finger on the light switch and one foot in the hallway when the office phone rang. Hoping it was Jenny calling to tell him her and her friends had arrived at the beach house early, Steven shot back to his desk and answered the phone.

"Archer, this is Dean Herbert. I need to see you. Can you stop by my office?"

Damn it!

Steven wished he had left the office thirty seconds sooner. "Sure, let me pull up my calendar. What do you need to meet with me about?"

"No, you don't understand. I need to see you right away. It will only take a few minutes. Can you stop by right now?"

"Sure, I was just heading home. I'll swing by in a few minutes. What is going—"

"Good." Without a goodbye, the dean hung up the phone.

Going to see Dr. Herbert was the last thing he wanted to do. He needed to get on the road to the beach house and start dinner for Jenny and her friends, but instead, Steven flopped down into his chair and sighed. He needed to compose himself before facing the man who had tried to get him fired.

Man, I wish Dr. Chester was still here instead of this flaming asshole.

The Dean of the College of Business, Dr. Alan R. Chester, had suffered a stroke a little less than a year before. Phillip Herbert, Ph.D., had been named acting dean. Since Dr. Chester went out on medical leave, Dr. Herbert had been running the College of Business, including the Computer Information Systems program in which Steven worked. Dr. Chester's health had not improved enough to return to his duties, and it was expected Dr. Herbert would be promoted to the permanent position of dean at the conclusion of the academic year.

An academic snob, Dr. Herbert detested professors hired from the private sector to teach at the university. He preached that a college professor should be a true academic with, at minimum, a doctorate degree. Dr. Herbert had let Steven's boss, the Computer Information Systems department head, know he did not consider Steven to be a true academic. He had remarked that Steven did not have enough formal, higher education to teach effectively at the university and had questioned the wisdom of renewing his contract for that year. Dr. Chester, who had adored and respected Steven, had not shared this opinion.

Fortunately, the other faculty members and staff in Steven's department, including the department head, had staunchly supported him, and the university renewed his contract.

Steven could think of only one reason why Dr. Herbert might want to meet with him in his office. As Frank had predicted, the shit had begun rolling down hill. The Chief of Police had probably played golf with the president of the university that morning. The Chief might have told the president about the previous night's murder and that the case potentially involved the WILCO Project. The president likely panicked and called the acting dean of the College of Business, Dr. Herbert, to alert him since the WILCO Project was part of the CIS program under his management. Dr. Herbert had just called Steven to his office, probably to find out what role the WILCO Project might have played in the case. If this were true, then the shit had parked itself at the bottom of the hill and possibly squarely on Steven's head.

Steven bolted from the chair and sprinted out of the computer center to the parking lot. He jumped into his sleek black sports car and drove the short distance to the administrative building, which housed the dean's office. The faculty rumor mill had churned out that Dr. Herbert had already moved into the dean's office even though the university had yet to officially award him the dean's job. Steven had been in the dean's office many times, but not since the acting dean had taken over the position and the office.

Steven bounded up a dozen granite steps, taking three at a stride and slipped into the front entrance of the nearly deserted College of Business building. Glancing at his watch, he hustled toward administrative offices located at the far end of the main hallway.

I don't have time for this, he thought as he approached the double doors leading to the suite that housed the administrative offices.

Pushing through the suite's heavy outer doors, he breezed past several deserted work areas, staffed during business hours by a shared pool of office assistants and approached the open door of the corner office. This, the most spacious office in the suite, was the dean's office.

Steven poked his head into the dean's office, and his mouth dropped open.

Is this the right office?

Jerking his head out of the doorway, he read the nameplate next to the door and verified that he had indeed come to the right place. He peered back into the dean's office, which looked nothing like it had when its former occupant, Dr. Chester, had been its resident. His office décor and furnishings had not been lavish, but Steven would have classified them as a definite step above the average department head's office.

The walls of the same office now featured premium, cherry wood paneling from floor to ceiling. Fancy crown molding adorned the seam where the walls met the ceiling.

An intricately carved chair rail graced the rich wood walls. Three of the room's walls displayed expensive art housed in elaborate frames. Dr. Herbert had exclusively dedicated the remaining wall to his vast array of meticulously matted and framed diplomas and academic certificates.

Pompass ass, Steven thought, shaking his head.

Light glistened off the newly varnished red oak hardwood floor. A sitting area, consisting of an overstuffed leather couch and two matching chairs placed around an ornate antique coffee table, all positioned on a large, expensive Persian rug, dominated the center of the large room.

Toward the rear of the room behind the sitting area sat a massive mahogany desk. An equally large high-backed, burgundy colored tufted leather chair loomed behind the gaudy desk, spun around so that its back faced the office door.

The little prick must have sunk at least fifty grand into this office.

He did not see the acting dean anywhere in the remodeled office. Clearing his throat, he rapped loudly on the doorframe.

The leather chair whirled around. Dr. Herbert nodded, but did not come around the enormous desk to

166

shake hands with Steven. Steven had not noticed him sitting in the chair before because he stood just over five feet tall and his head did not reach the top of the high-backed chair. Extremely overweight, the dean's rotund body appeared nearly as wide as he was tall.

The dean's dyed black hair was longer than the current style, over the ears and touching his collar in the back, but neatly trimmed. He wore tiny wire-rimmed glasses perched on his small wide nose. His closely trimmed goatee, also obviously dyed black, extended well below his chin onto his puffy jowls.

Being a Saturday, Steven had expected Dr. Herbert to be dressed casually. Steven himself wore shorts, a polo shirt and sandals. Instead of wearing khakis and a long sleeve dress shirt as Steven had guessed, Dr. Herbert dressed exactly as he would have for a regular workday. He wore a tan, lightweight summer suit over a starched, white Oxford dress shirt with the knot of his perfectly matched striped tie cinched tightly, as if he were about to step into a job interview.

"Archer, thanks for coming by." Dr. Herbert always referred to Steven by his last name only, a not-so-subtle attempt at a put down.

"No trouble. What can I do for you, Dr. Herbert?"

"I received a call this afternoon from the president of the university. He was quite agitated about this business of the body that was found on campus this morning. Are you aware of this situation?"

"I am," Steven replied.

"So, what can you tell me?" Dr. Herbert demanded, squeezing out of his chair. He leaned across the desk and stared at Steven.

"With all due respect, sir, nothing. The police have forbidden me from speaking with anyone about the case."

"I see. I was told the victim was playing a game you and your students are developing. Some sort of cell phone game? Is that true?"

"I'm sorry, Dr. Herbert, but I am not at liberty to discuss the case with you."

Dr. Herbert's face turned red as he pawed at the lower portion of his goatee.

"Fine. Let me tell you what I know. The poor girl that was killed last night was playing your game. That means you *are* involved in this case. Because you work for me, *I* am now involved in this case."

Dr. Herbert paused and pointed a Steven. "Let me spell this out for you, Archer. If this game of yours had anything to do with the murder, you are responsible. Since

168

you work in the College of Business, I am also then responsible. So let me ask you one more time, was the girl playing the game last night?"

"You obviously already know the answer to that question, since you just told me you did, so why ask me?" Steven responded. "I have been told not to discuss this case with anyone, period."

Steven could see the fury in Dr. Herbert's eyes, yet he calmly stepped back to his chair and boosted himself up into the seat. Steven nearly laughed aloud as the short, fat man struggled to climb into the chair.

Dr. Herbert whipped around and grinned at Steven.

"Now you listen to me, Archer. You had better hope this game of yours did not put that innocent young lady in the woods so that some nutcase could kill her. I do not want to have to explain to the president and the Board of Regents why a university-sponsored project was responsible for one of our students getting killed."

He glared at Steven for a couple of seconds then continued. "Something like this would have never happened if I had been in charge. This is an institution of higher learning. We are not supposed to be doing commercial projects, we should be doing research and publishing. If this project of yours brings any disgrace to this university I will shut it down immediately."

"Is that all?" Steven asked, trying to appear nonchalant.

"No. I don't care for your attitude, Archer. Dr. Chester allowed you to be hired, but he is no longer in charge here." Dr. Herbert raised both hands and gazed around the palatial office. "If you and your project cause me trouble, I will not hesitate to remove you from this faculty. That is all."

Without a word, Steven left the dean's office and trotted to his car.

Gunning the engine, he exited the campus and made his way to the interstate. He drove south on the highway, heading for the beach house. He tuned the car stereo to a classic rock station and cranked the volume, trying to forget about the conversation with Dr. Herbert.

Dr. Herbert had been looking for a reason to fire Steven, and this case could provide him with the perfect reason to let him go. Christina had definitely been playing the WILCO Project game at the time she was killed. Steven had seen the game still active on her phone himself. That, however, did not mean the game had caused her death. Steven knew he had to prove the game had not directly caused Christina's demise—his job at the university depended on it.

Chapter Sixteen

Saturday, November 8 -- 6:28 P.M.

Jonathan felt like a new man after finally catching up on some much-needed sleep that afternoon. Excited that his date had gone well so far, he could not stop smiling at Amanda Harvey. Her blue eyes sparkled with reflected candlelight as she blew lightly on a spoonful of her steaming, chocolate soufflé. She guided the bite of soufflé into her mouth and then eased the spoon out.

"Oh my God, this is almost as good as sex," she said, eyes closed, savoring the taste of the rich dessert.

"Almost better than sex? Are you saying you're not a virgin?"

Amanda offered him a devilish smile. "Daddy thinks I'm still a virgin. You gotta try this." She dipped the spoon back into the dessert.

Jonathan drained the last bit of *Merlot* from his glass and lifted the bottle, eager for a refill. A frown replaced his beaming smile as he realized it was empty. He had consumed the entire bottle himself and the warm, numbing effect of the alcohol had hit his brail full force. He stared back at Amanda who had just started sipping her fifth *Cosmopolitan* martini, and he knew she, too, was drunk.

The beautiful girl pursed her lips and exhaled a stream of cool air toward another bite of steaming cake. Jonathan inhaled the heavy aroma of chocolate laced with vodka and cranberry from the martinis. She inched the spoon toward him and, just as he began closing his mouth, she pulled the spoon back. Giggling, she teased him a couple more times and then finally let him taste the soufflé.

"Oh, you're right, that is good, but it's not better than sex."

With Amanda continuing to feed Jonathan, they alternated bites until they finished the dessert. Leaning back, Amanda closed her eyes.

"I am so full. The food was excellent, especially that dessert." Swallowing the last of her Cosmo, she grabbed her purse. "I need to go to the ladies' room. I'll be right back."

Smiling warmly, Amanda stood, steadied herself, and then headed to the restroom. Jonathan stared at her as she strutted like a runway model away from the table.

God, she is gorgeous.

He closed his eyes and imagined her naked.

"Jonathan, it's good to see you again. Was everything all right this evening?"

The question, delivered with a heavy Italian accent, brought Jonathan back from his fantasy. Jonathan smiled and shook hands with his friend and the owner of the restaurant, Mr. Giglio.

"Oh, yes, everything was fantastic as usual, Mr. Giglio. How are you doing?"

"Damn football games." He motioned around the nearly empty restaurant. Several idle waiters and waitresses milled around the beverage station spinning their serving trays and talking with each other. "You Americans are obsessed with that stupid game. Why do you have to have football games on Saturday evening? My best night is ruined."

Mr. Giglio started to place a tip tray with the bill on the table, but before he could set it down, Jonathan handed him a credit card. Mr. Giglio nodded toward the beverage station and snapped his fingers. In a second, one of the waiters took the bill and credit card and disappeared.

"I hadn't noticed, but now that you mention it, the place is pretty empty."

"Oh well, what are you going to do? I see you are dining with a most beautiful girl tonight. Are you on a date?"

"Yeah."

"Good for you. I haven't seen much of you since you and Christina, you know, anyway, it's good to see you happy and with such a pretty girl."

Amanda arrived back at the table sporting a fresh coat of lipstick and Jonathan stood.

"Mr. Giglio, this is Amanda. Amanda, this is the owner of this fine restaurant."

The distinguished looking older man took Amanda's hand in his and gave it a quick kiss. In return, Amanda flashed him one of her heart-stopping smiles.

"Oh, how sweet. It's very nice to meet you. Dinner was excellent."

"I am glad you kids liked it. I must go, but I hope to see the both of you back again real soon."

Mr. Giglio released Amanda's hand, bowed his head and then left the table. Jonathan quickly signed the credit card slip.

"Are you ready?" he asked Amanda.

"Yes. Thanks for dinner, I had a great time." Smiling at Jonathan, she grabbed his hand, and they exited the restaurant and headed for the car. Remembering the test-game would start at seven, Jonathan checked his watch, noting it was almost six o'clock.

"I need to stop by my place and grab my team hat for the game. You brought yours, right?"

"Yep, it's in the car."

Jonathan escorted her to the passenger door of his car, but instead of reaching for the door handle, he pivoted, positioning himself between her and the car, with his back against the car door.

He gently caressed her cheek and positioned her long blonde hair behind her ear. She closed her eyes. Using the back of his hand, he gently stroked her cheek. She moaned softly. Cupping her face, he moved in close. Her eyes still closed, her breath quickened.

Now it's my turn to tease!

He gently brushed his lips over hers, barely touching her. She tried to kiss him back but he pulled his face away from her. He pushed her hair behind her ear, exposing her neck. He softly kissed her neck, beginning from her shoulder then moving all the way up to her ear.

She placed her hands on his hips and tried to pull his body close to her, but he held her back. Goose bumps covered her arms and her erect nipples showed through her top. Eyes still closed, she moaned again.

Breathing heavily, he gently nipped at her earlobe with his teeth. A slight tremor moved through her body. She tried again to pull him close, but he resisted, not allowing her body to touch his. He blew softly into her ear and then lightly traced the outline of her ear with the tip of his tongue, beginning at the lobe then working up and around the top.

Frustration etching a delicate wrinkle above her closed eyes, she moaned again and moved her hand from his waist to her own breast. He softly flicked his tongue in and out of her ear. She squeezed her breast and rolled her nipple between her thumb and forefinger. Her breathing became rapid and her body shook.

Her body shuddering harder, he pulled her close to him and put his lips to hers and her tongue hungrily entered his mouth. Releasing her breast and grabbing his hips with both hands, she ground her crotch against his thigh, kissing him deeply.

After a few seconds, the trembling in her body quieted. She pulled her face away from his and opened her eyes.

"It's never happened like that before," she whispered. Jonathan smiled, not knowing what to say. She pulled his face toward hers. Still breathing heavily, she whispered in his ear, "I want you. Let's go to your place, now."

***

Approaching the auditorium, Bobbi Cline surveyed the steps already crowded with students, all carrying cell phones and wearing or holding black baseball caps. She glanced at her watch, which read six-thirty. She had arrived a half-hour early for the start of the WILCO Project test-game and there must have been forty kids already milling about. She could hardly believe the turnout considering the telecast of the big football game would begin in minutes.

Scattered groups of students dotted the steps leading to the entrance of the auditorium. The crowd appeared upbeat and excited with the din of the students' chatter

178

punctuated by laughter and occasional shouts. One larger cluster of students consisted of several new players grouped around an obvious game veteran, who lectured about strategy and doled out hints and tips to the newbies like Yoda passing on the ways of the Jedi.

Based on the crowd's mood, Bobbi guessed none of the students had heard about the previous night's tragedy that had occurred on campus. She wondered how many of them would still be so eager to play the game that night if they knew about the murder.

The nagging question of why Professor Archer had become involved with the case stormed back into her head. She theorized that the crime had to be somehow related to the internet, or it involved the WILCO Project. If the murder had something to do with the game, then she or any of the other players about to participate were potential victims. A chill ran down her spine and she held off an urge to bolt to the top of the steps shouting to everyone that the project team had canceled the game and to go home.

With the sun beginning to set over the auditorium's ornate granite façade, Bobbi casually cruised through the groups of players looking into their faces, wondering if one of them belonged to a cold-blooded killer. She felt for her ever-present notebook stuffed in the right, rear pocket of her jeans. She quickly patted the other rear pocket and fingered the bulge of the small can of mace she had decided to bring with her.

Better safe than sorry!

***

Jonathan and Amanda burst into his apartment, lips locked and hands groping. He immediately led her through the living room, down the short hallway and into his dark bedroom. He lay down on the bed, face up and pulled her on top of him. Face flushed, she thrust both hands on his chest and pushed herself up so she straddled him.

"Wait here," she commanded.

The bad girl expression returned to her face, and she jumped up and slipped out of the room.

Left alone in the dark room, hard with anticipation, Jonathan wondering what she had in mind. Had she chickened out and planned to ditch him? After all, she seemed satisfied after their little encounter in the restaurant parking lot. Holding his breath, he listened intently for the sound of the front door opening...nothing.

He began pushing himself up on his elbows to get out of bed and find her when he heard the toilet flushing.

180

He let out a huge sigh of relief and flopped back down on the bed. A few seconds later, she came back to the bedroom doorway, holding one of his kitchen chairs.

"Can you turn on some music?" she asked.

"Music? Sure." He rolled over to the far nightstand and turned on the clock radio. The latest hit from Britney Spears streamed from the speakers. "Is this okay?"

"Turn it up a little and turn on the lamps."

Jonathan cranked up the volume and flipped on each of the lamps that sat on matching nightstands on either side of the bed. She tripped the wall switch by the door turning on the overhead light, brightly illuminating the bedroom.

Jonathan grinned and stared at Amanda's hips, which had begun subtly gyrating to the beat of the music. She placed the kitchen chair sideways, just inside the doorway. She kicked off her shoes, but was otherwise fully clothed. Jonathan rose back up on his elbows and began moving toward her when she, still undulating seductively to the music, shook her head and pointed to the head of the bed. He sat up with his back against the headboard, hypnotized by her swaying body.

She wore a white split neck tee shirt with the *DKNY Jeans* logo across the chest. The short sleeveless shirt left her midriff bare and it clung to the curves of her chest and torso like a second skin. She had on tiny, white cargo-style shorts with a matching wide, grommeted belt, which she had unbuckled and left open. The shorts rode so low on her hips that the space between her pierced belly button and the snap on her shorts seemed to go on forever. The contrast between the bright white outfit and her deeply tanned skin heightened her sexy look.

Hips swaying to the beat of the music, she placed her right foot up on the seat of the chair, accentuating her long, shapely leg. She touched her fingertips to her knees then slowly traced her fingernails up her thighs and across her crotch. She continued moving her fingertips across her bare, flat stomach and traced along the outside of her breasts, her thumbs rubbing over her hard nipples. With the tops of her fingernails, she continued tracing up her chest and along her neck to her ears. She completed the maneuver by combing her fingers through her long blonde hair and tossing her head back in perfect rhythm with the beat of the music.

She unsnapped her shorts and unzipped them just enough to reveal the top of her white panties. Body swaying, she slowly peeled off the tee shirt leaving her

182

upper body naked except for her white satin bra and a gold necklace with "Amanda" in script around her neck.

Placing her foot back on the floor she slid off her shorts. Smiling at Jonathan, she put her hands on the chair and pivoted so her back faced him. Her long blonde hair fell down across her back ending just above the bra strap. Her low-rise, thong style panties showed off the rounded cheeks of her perfect rear end.

Hips moving to the music, she looked back over her shoulder at Jonathan. Smiling back at her, he mouthed, "Wow." Still moving to the rhythm of the music, she finally joined him in bed where she made it worth the wait.

Chapter Seventeen

Saturday, November 8 -- 11:53 P.M.

Bobbi Cline pressed her back against the outside rear wall of a campus equipment building. The building blocked any light from the street leaving the area pitch black. A few yards beyond her, a stand of tall trees surrounded the back and sides of the building. The corrugated metal building housed tractors and other maintenance equipment. She had positioned herself at the center of the rectangular building's seventy-foot rear wall. Her sweat-soaked shirt clung to her body as rivulets of sweat ran down her arms and dripped off her elbows. She wanted to keep moving, but needed to stop for a minute and catch her breath. She squinted into the murky shadows, searching for signs of movement, while making sure to scan her cell phone display every second or so.

She looked at her watch. It was nearly midnight and somehow she had survived elimination from the game. She exhaled. According to her phone's radar display, whoever had chased her to this hiding place had given up. She smiled.

Looks like I finally lost the bastard.

The game had rendered her both physically and mentally exhausted, but she managed a fist pump.

Not bad for a rookie—I could actually win this game, she thought with a smile. But the smile of satisfaction quickly turned into a frown as she reminded herself that a killer could be lurking in the dark shadows of the campus.

She snapped back to reality as the border around her phone's display flashed red.

Damn it!

Enemy radar had lit her up again. She studied the display and saw that the bad guy had moved to the center of the building's front side. That placed her enemy about fifty feet away, at roughly the same spot she stood, but on the opposite side of the building.

The red flashing border on her phone stopped, indicating the enemy had turned off their radar, which also caused the enemy's icon to vanish from her map. Her pulse rate shot up as she realized her opponent planned to attack her from one side of the building or the other.

Which side is the bastard gonna pick?

Taking a guess, she sprinted to the right rear corner of the building and stopped. She quickly flicked on her radar and focused intently on the screen to see which way her opponent had moved. The bad guy had chosen the opposite route and now moved along the left side of the building toward the rear wall. She turned off her radar to stop broadcasting her position and held still for a second, listening for the enemy.

Suddenly, a brilliant flash exploded from the trees to her right, opposite the building, momentarily blinding her. She heard footsteps running toward her and then another bright flash went off. A guy from the other team rushed toward her only a few yards away, phone to face, ready to shoot again.

She raised her phone to her eye and tried to line up a shot on the enemy rushing her from the trees, but she was too late. Her phone began playing the notes of a death march and the screen showed a picture of a tombstone with her game name, "NewsHound", printed across the front. The enemy had captured and eliminated her from the game.

"Shit!" she murmured, partly upset that her foe had outplayed her, but also relieved that the enemy was just another gamer and not a crazed murderer.

The guy from the trees that scored the hit let out a hoot and yelled to his partner on the opposite side of the building, "I got her! I got her! Get over here!"

They'd tricked her. The two guys teamed up and had worked together to capture her. The first guy on the opposite side of the building occupied her attention, while his partner ambushed her from the trees opposite the building.

The guy from the other side of the building jogged up to Bobbi and the shooter.

"We got you! Great shot, Brad," the first guy said.

"Yeah, nice going. I never saw you coming," Bobbie said to the shooter.

"That's the way it's supposed to work. Chad keeps you busy, while I finish you off," the shooter said.

"The Brad and Chad Show," Bobbi said, smiling at them. Sweat dripping down her face, she shook her head, "You guys make a good team. I'm Bobbi." They all shook hands.

"Well, you put up a good fight, Bobbi. We've been stalking you for quite a while," Brad said.

"Is this your first time?" Chad asked.

"It is," Bobbi replied, removing her glasses and wiping her face with the back of her arm.

"You did pretty good for a newbie. You can play on our team anytime," Chad said.

"We'd love to stay and chat but we've got bad guys to kill. Come on, let's go," Brad said.

"All right, nice meeting you guys, except for the killing part," Bobbi answered. They all laughed, and the boys ran off to finish the game.

Bobbi, tired and sweaty, headed for home. She could not believe how intense playing the WILCO Project game had been.

What a blast! No wonder everyone on campus raved about it.

She'd gained a new appreciation for how Navy submarine captains must feel as they patrol the oceans, searching for the enemy. The game had not been as easy to master as she had thought because actively searching for opponents with the radar also advertised your own position.

Mentally spent from being on edge for nearly four hours straight, she could hardly wait to take a long shower and collapse into her bed. The game had been a good diversion from thinking about the murder. Now, with the game over, her mind immediately refocused on the case. Even though exhausted from playing the game, Bobbi realized sleep would not come easily that night because she knew a real killer still ran loose on campus.

Chapter Eighteen

Sunday, November 9 -- 11:12 A.M.

Sitting on the large, second story deck of his house overlooking the white sandy beaches of the Gulf of Mexico, Steven closed his eyes and exhaled, thankful he had a place he could escape and enjoy guaranteed relaxation. No matter what in his life caused him stress, he could always count on the rhythmic sound of the waves breaking on the beach and the constant cool sea breezes to return a level of peace to his being.

Even though he had made millions in the technology boom of the dot-com era, purchasing this beach house had been his only real extravagance.

Okay, he admitted, *this house and my black, convertible Porsche 911 Carrera.*

Much too big for just himself, the house consisted of a master suite plus four guest bedrooms which he shared with family and friends.

190

Steven took a deep breath of fresh, salty sea air and surveyed the beach. Late on a Sunday morning, crowds of people had invaded the white sandy expanse below. They all seemed carefree as they sunbathed, built sandcastles and romped in the surf. They'd chosen the perfect fall day for a beach outing with the temperature in the low eighties and not a cloud in the sky.

He had just finished feeding Jenny and her five girlfriends a huge breakfast of pancakes and sausages. Making good on his vow, the girls had remained in his sight the entire night. Keeping an eye on them had not been a difficult task as he had stuffed them with a huge dinner of grilled steaks and shrimp, baked potatoes and salad. By halfway through the second movie they had all fallen asleep, obviously worn out from their day of canoeing on the river.

Steven watched the girls leave the house and make their way down the sandy path, through the wild sea oats, toward the sparkling waves to claim their spot on the beach and bask in the sun. Jenny turned and waved to him. It seemed like only yesterday that as a chubby toddler he bounced her on his knee while she squealed with delight. He had watched her grow from a freckle-faced tomboy, who never went anywhere without her Atlanta Braves baseball cap jammed over her curly red hair, into a beautiful, popular, intelligent young woman. He smiled and waved back to her, unable to bear the thought of how awful he would feel if some monster suddenly stole her away from him and the rest of the family.

Steven opened the Sunday paper half expecting the front page headline to read something like, "Student Slain on University Campus." He heaved a sigh of relief when he saw an unrelated headline and found no story about the murder on the front page at all.

Frank must have gotten to Bobbi Cline. He quickly glanced through the remainder of the main section and the Metro section and found no mention of an incident on campus. He found it hard to believe no one from the press had gotten wind of the crime.

Normally extremely responsive, it seemed out of character for Jonathan to not return Steven's calls. Throughout the project, Jonathan had not hesitated to get back to him any time of the day, on nights and on weekends, yet he had not talked to him in nearly twenty-four hours. Had Jonathan disappeared? Maybe he had *lost it*, like he had with Patricia at the game orientation meeting, but on a much bigger scale with Christina. Could losing it with Christina have included committing the unthinkable in the woods Friday night?

On impulse, he picked up his cell phone and dialed Jonathan's cell phone number. If Jonathan answered, would he have the courage to confront him about the murder? He could think of no good reasons to confront him. If Jonathan was indeed the killer, accusing him could seriously jeopardize the authorities' ability to catch him. Steven might also be putting himself, Jenny or others in danger.

Jonathan did not answer his cell phone. The voicemail greeting came on without a single ring, which meant he had probably turned his cell phone off. Steven left another message for him to call back. No sooner had he finish leaving it than his cell phone rang. Steven looked at the caller ID and saw the name *Diaz.*

"Frank, good morning."

"Hi Steven, nothing good about this morning."

"What's wrong?"

"You at the beach?"

"Yeah, I had Jenny and a few of her friends stay here last night. I wanted to keep an eye on her."

"You didn't say anything about the murder?"

"No. I didn't mention a thing."

"Good."

"What's going on, Frank?"

"I need you to come back to campus right away. We've found another body."

Chapter Nineteen

The killer had struck again.

Shit, another body.

Steven slapped his hand on the table and chewed his lower lip. Frank relayed to Steven the location of the crime scene and then they hung up. Jumping up from the table, Steven hurried downstairs. He sprinted out of the back door and down to the beach, frantically looking for Jenny and her friends.

After searching for what seemed like several minutes, Steven found the girls. Before addressing them, he paused to catch his breath and gain his composure.

"Hey, Jenny."

"Hi, Uncle Steven, what's up?"

"Listen, I've got to go back to the campus right away."

"Okay, do you need us to pack up and head back?"

"No, no, please stay."

"It's okay, we were going to head back in a little while anyway. Is everything okay? You look...I don't know, are you feeling okay?"

She was either very perceptive, or Steven had done a terrible job of hiding his emotions. Trying hard to appear calm, he offered her weak smile. "I'm fine."

With an apparent serial killer loose, Steven was not about to allow Jenny and her friends to return to campus. Screw Frank and his orders to keep this quiet. He knelt facing the group.

"Girls, there's something I need to talk to you about." Jenny and her friends, lying in row on beach towels, propped themselves up on their elbows and looked intently at Steven. Cautiously looking around, he lowered his voice and continued. "I am going to tell you something, but first I want you to promise me two things, okay?"

Eyes wide, the girls all nodded their heads in agreement.

"First, what I am going to tell you is a bit shocking so I need you all to remain calm. Please don't make a big scene. Second, I want you to keep what I'm about to tell you to yourselves for now. Do not tell anyone until I let you know it is okay to talk about it. Does everyone understand?"

Again, all six heads nodded. Steven took a deep breath. "Okay, there have been two bodies found on campus, one Saturday morning and one this morning." Several of the girls gasped. They all murmured similar questions at the same time.

Steven held both hands up, and the girls stopped talking. "I know you all have questions, so I'm going to tell you everything I can about what's going on."

Steven told the girls about Christina Howard, leaving out many of the details, including her identity.

"I don't know anything about the second body because I just got the call from the police a few minutes ago. I need to get back to campus as soon as possible. You girls are safe here at the beach, but I'm going to have the police put a car outside the house just in case. Go back to the house, lock the doors and windows, and set the alarm. You know the code, right, Jenny?"

Jenny nodded.

"Don't let anyone into the house. There's plenty of food. You should have everything you need. If there are any problems or you need something, call my cell. I want you to promise me you will stay here. Do not go back to campus, okay?"

The girls all agreed, and Steven stood to leave. Jabbering nervously, the girls started packing up to return to the house. Their faces all had expressions of fear and shock. Steven pulled Jenny aside, out of earshot of the others.

"Jenny, I need you to be a leader, can you do that?"

"Yeah, sure." Her lower lip quivered. He smiled and patted her cheek.

"Good. Don't go back to campus and whatever you do, do not let anyone in the house except me or your parents or the police, okay?"

"Okay."

"That includes anyone from my project team."

"Okay."

"Everything is going to be fine. I've got to go."

She reached up and gave him a strong hug.

"Be safe, Uncle Steven."

"I will, promise."

Waving to the girls, Steven sprinted back to the house. Within fifteen minutes, he had navigated through the coastal town and inland to the interstate heading north toward campus.

Fortunately, the thicker traffic clogged the southbound lanes of the highway as the majority of the crowds still headed toward the beach, leaving his lanes toward the city relatively clear. Keeping his eye on his trusty radar detector, he settled in the left lane of the highway and pushed the *Porsche* to ninety.

Steven pulled out his cell phone and dialed Frank.

"Steven, where are you?" Frank asked.

"I'm on the interstate. I'll be there in less than thirty minutes."

"Good."

"Frank, I need you to put a car outside my beach house. I've got Jenny and her friends holed up there. I want someone to keep an eye on her and the house to make sure nothing bad happens."

"Yeah, good idea. Consider it done. I gotta go. I'll see you when you get here."

Getting Frank to agree to assign a squad car to watch the beach house had been too easy. Steven had expected Frank to push back on his request with excuses about jurisdiction or lack of manpower. Frank must have had a good reason to keep an eye on Jenny. He, too, must have believed she was potentially in danger.

Steven pressed the sports car to nearly one hundred miles an hour. Frank's willingness to protect Jenny with a patrol car meant he thought her life could be at risk, and he did not want to take any chances. In a moment of realization, Steven slammed his hand on the steering wheel —he was the link. There must be something at the new crime scene that involved the WILCO Project game.

Steven darted in and out of traffic, needing to get to the crime scene as quickly as possible. He suspected Frank had found a clue tying the murder directly to the game. Given the mounting evidence against Jonathan, Steven feared that Frank had surely found further evidence pointing to Jonathan as the killer.

***

Jolted awake by the sound of her ringing cell phone, Bobbi Cline bolted upright in her bed. The phone had awoken her in the midst of a terrifying dream. In the dream, she had been playing in one of Professor Archer's cell phone games, chased by the campus killer. The harder she tried to run, the slower she went. At every turn in the chase, ridiculous obstacles prevented her from fleeing the murderer. With every frustrating step, her nemesis drew closer.

A well-meaning child had given her a bicycle, but the chain kept coming off. She finally fixed the chain, and then the tires flattened, one at a time. Ditching the useless bike, she fled the killer on foot. The sidewalks suddenly turned from a normal, hard slab to sticky, newly poured concrete. Her legs churned, but she made little forward progress, bogged down in the wet concrete. Just as the faceless killer's hand jabbed out to grab her, the sound of her cell phone woke her up.

Heart racing, she opened her eyes. It took a couple of seconds for her to realize no killer had been chasing her, and she sat safely in her bed. Feeling exhausted, she felt her damp hair plastered to her forehead and her over-sized tee shirt, soaked with sweat, clinging to her body.

She took a deep breath, and she glanced at her bedside clock radio, hardly believing it was already almost noon on Sunday. She answered the ringing cell phone.

"Ms. Cline? Detective Frank Diaz here."

"Yes, hello Detective Diaz."

"Ms. Cline, have you seen the paper today?"

Oh shit!

Had someone leaked the story? If yesterday's murder had made the city paper, she had lost her scoop. Even worse, Detective Diaz would unfairly blame her for leaking the story. "Um, no, I haven't."

"I want you to know that I am a man of my word, Ms. Cline, and we had a deal."

"Yes, we did, and I just want you to know I didn't say a word to anyone." She gritted her teeth because she knew he was about to chew her head off.

"And I just want to say thanks for keeping yesterday's incident out of the paper. I know it must have been hard for you to sit on the story. I asked you to trust me, and you did. I really appreciate it."

"You're welcome," Bobbi mumbled, letting her head fall back on the pillow and exhaling.

"Being a man of my word, I'm going to hold up my side of the bargain. Are you close to campus?"

"Yes, my apartment is just off campus."

"There's been another incident. Can you come to the scene?"

"Yes, absolutely."

"You know where they are putting up that new building, on the opposite side of campus from the last scene?"

"Yes."

"Okay, get over here as soon as you can. The crime scene is at the construction site. Don't go waving around your press credentials. If the brass finds out I am dealing with the press directly, we're both in big trouble."

"Okay, no press card, how will I—"

"Just tell the uniforms that I requested you at the scene and to come and get me. You got it, Ms. Cline?"

"Got it, I'll be right there. Oh, Detective Diaz, you can call me Bobbi."

"I'll see you when you get here, Ms. Cline," he shot back curtly and hung up the phone.

Chapter Twenty

Sunday, November 9 -- 11:58 A.M.

Bobbi jumped out of bed and turned on the shower, adrenaline pumping through her body. Just like a real investigative reporter, she was going to an actual crime scene. Not just any crime scene, but the scene of a murder.

Honoring his word, Detective Diaz had called her to the scene so she could break the story of the campus murders. She pictured the headline "*2 Dead in Campus Slayings*", and more importantly, "*by Bobbi Cline*".

Chewing her lower lip, Bobbi's excitement turned to trepidation. The scene she was about to visit would have a dead person's body. She had never seen a real dead body. The person, likely a fellow student about her age, would be a victim of murder, with the killer still at large. A chill ran through her body.

"Why had Detective Diaz taken a chance on getting me involved?" she wondered aloud. Partly because of her threat, he clearly did not want her to break the story too early. Diaz involved her because he planned to feed her the exact information he wanted the public to know. He probably assumed that, because of her youth and inexperience, she would never think of double-crossing him and releasing unapproved information. He trusted her, which was why he decided to use her in this case. She could help him.

Detective Diaz could use her all he wanted to, she did not care. Bobbi smiled. Tomorrow she would file the biggest story ever to run in the school newspaper's history, tagged with her name in the byline. She would be scooping the city paper and local TV news teams because she had become the unofficial mouthpiece for the police. Detective Diaz would give her details no other reporter would get. Eager to get to the crime scene, Bobbi jumped into the steaming shower.

***

After parking the *Porsche*, Steven jogged a half a block to the crime scene. Unlike yesterday morning, groups of onlookers, mostly students, milled about, talking and pointing at the building, held back by wooden barricades.

Unfortunately for Frank, this crime could not be kept secret. The cat was out of the bag.

The barricades lined the front of the half-constructed building, positioned in the sand between the street and the freshly poured concrete sidewalk. Construction junk and trash littered a fifteen-foot section of sand just beyond the new sidewalk. Scrap wood of all shapes and sizes, used sidewalk forms, broken cinder blocks, enough Big Gulp cups and Gatorade bottles to hydrate the football team, and a potpourri of fast food wrappers lay scattered everywhere.

The building would eventually be three stories high when completed, according to the picture on the sign the construction company had placed at the front of the lot. The external walls were only partially completed, but builders had laid enough concrete to limit the view into the building's interior.

Two smallish oak trees stood on either side of the building's entrance. Yellow crime scene tape stretched across the front of the structure, from the building's left corner, around the oak trees and all the way to the opposite corner.

Four uniformed police officers, stationed behind the barricades between the street and the building, faced the street. Steven approached the middle barricade where two of the cops talked with each other while constantly eyeing the growing group of onlookers. One cop, tall and skinny, cupped a half-smoked cigarette in his hand while his short and husky partner stood next to him, shifting his weight from one leg to the other, sweating profusely.

"Excuse me guys, I'm Steven Archer. I'm here to see Detective Frank Diaz."

The shorter cop nodded at Steven and pulled his radio off his belt.

"Sarge, I got a Steven Archer out front here to see Diaz. Over."

"Roger. I'll let him know. Out."

"Hang tight, they're letting him know you're here," the short one said, as if Steven had been unable to hear the sergeant's reply over the radio.

A minute later Frank appeared in the building's doorway. "Steven. Guys, let him through, he's okay."

Steven dodged around the barricade and met Frank halfway through the junkyard between the sidewalk and the building, just inside the crime scene tape. They shook hands.

"Steven, thanks for coming," Frank said, keeping his voice low.

"What have you got here?"

"Some teenagers were horsing around in the building this morning when they stumbled onto victim number two."

Steven shook his head at Frank and let out a long breath. He looked back toward the street and nodded at the crowd.

"No chance of keeping this one quiet, is there?"

"Not hardly. The news crews are already on the way."

A young woman's desperate voice emanated from beyond the barricade Steven had just passed through.

"But he said to tell you guys to get him," the woman pleaded, the volume of her voice rising with each word. "He's right there—Detective Diaz!" Shouting now, she waved at Frank.

"What the hell is she doing here?" Steven asked, after recognizing Bobbi Cline.

"It's okay. I'm going to give her the story. I'll explain later." Frank glanced toward Bobbi. "She's okay, guys. Let her through," Frank called to the Laurel and Hardy shaped uniforms. The fat one shrugged his shoulders and moved the barricade back, allowing Bobbi to slip through it.

"Ms. Cline, thanks for coming," Frank said, his voice low again. "You two know each other already, or so I've heard."

Steven and Bobbi exchanged nods. Frank led them to the doorway, but stopped before taking them inside the building.

"We've identified the victim as Amanda Harvey. She's a student, a freshman." He looked at Bobbi who scribbled furiously in her notepad. "Can't use her name yet, we're still notifying her next of kin. We found her cell phone and the hat. Same deal as yesterday."

"Cell phone and hat. What deal? What are you talking about?" Bobbi asked, her eyebrows cocked in confusion.

"You mean she was..." Steven began to answer then hesitated, looking at Frank for approval to continue. Frank gave him an almost imperceptible nod, and Steven kept talking, "So she was playing the game when she was killed. What about a 911 call?"

"Same thing as before," Frank replied. "A 911 call was made from the victim's cell phone. It was a hang up. The E911 location data showed the call originating from the dog track on the other side of town."

"I don't get it. Was the 911 call made from here or the dog track?" Bobbi asked.

Steven explained to Bobbi what had happened with the 911 call and the incorrect location data with the previous murder.

"So let me get this straight," Bobbi said. "This victim, Amanda Harvey, was playing the WILCO Project game when she got attacked by the killer. She tried to dial 911. The call got through but the killer grabbed the phone before she could talk to the operator and hung up. But because the call got through, the 911 operator was able to get the location from where the call was dialed."

Steven nodded in agreement, so Bobbi went on. "The computer said the location of the call was the dog track even though you are pretty sure the call was made right from here? How can that be?"

"We're not sure," Frank answered. "That's what we are trying to figure out."

"Frank, we logged on to the LBS server at USA Wireless yesterday and determined there are three people involved in the project who had accessed the system over the past month, both Jonathan and Patricia from the university and Larry Hershman, who works for USA Wireless," Steven said. "If someone were manipulating the

LBS location data it would have to be done on that LBS server. The computer physically sits in the USA Wireless data center, since that's where the location data that feeds the E911 system comes from."

"So you are telling me Jonathan, Patricia and this Hershman guy have all been accessing the LBS server?" Frank asked. "That means they all have access to the computer that provides the location data. They all have had the opportunity to manipulate it."

"Correct." Steven answered. "Just keep in mind Patricia wrote the LBS interface using Larry's support on the USA Wireless end."

"Who is this Hershman guy?" asked Frank.

"Larry Hershman is the project manager from USA Wireless who is assigned to work with our project team," Steven answered.

"Okay, but what do you really know about him?" Frank asked. "Should we be concerned about this guy? I mean he is accessing the computer that is giving out bogus locations, right?"

"Larry's a strange guy," Steven answered. "I've gotten to know him pretty well while working on this project. He's had a tough year both at home and at work.

I've had a few heart to hearts with him. I'm not sure he has many friends outside of work."

"So what's his story?" Frank probed further.

"Larry started working for the local phone company, climbing poles, right out of high school, just like his dad." Steven answered. "He's a bright and ambitious guy, and he got tired and bored with his job. Fixing phone service outages was no longer a challenge for him. He had always been intrigued by computers, but knew nothing about them since he had never gone to college—this was in the early seventies, way before you could call Dell and get a PC shipped directly to your house. The only computers around back then were big water-cooled mainframes."

"So how does a lineman for the phone company learn computers?" Frank asked.

"He applied for an internal training program at the phone company's Data Services division to learn how to program mainframe computers," Steven answered. "Entrance in the program was highly selective and extremely competitive. He passed the entrance exams and made it into the program."

"So the company retrained him," Bobbi interjected.

"That's right," Steven said. "The program lasted three months and he said it was like taking a year and a half of advanced college classes in a single quarter. He learned computer programming and systems analysis and design. He told me it was brutal and there were several times he almost quit. He stayed with it and passed the final exam. His scores made him the top trainee in his class. He was highly recruited and had his pick of the various development projects. He became an excellent systems programmer, and his career really took off."

"Sounds like this guy was dead set on getting ahead," Frank said.

"He was and did. He rose to the rank of senior manager, always taking on the toughest and most critical projects. You know, the ones nobody else wanted to tackle. He consistently delivered, giving him the reputation as the "go-to-guy" in the organization. Then he began noticing others he had worked alongside, and in some cases had trained, being promoted above him. He could not earn a promotion to the next level. He said management kept making promises like "Get this project done and fix this mess, and you'll get the promotion.""

"Lemme guess, no promotion," Frank said.

"That's right," Steven said. "The promotion never came. Management finally told him that his lack of a college degree was holding him back. So, he tried taking college courses at night, but it was impossible. He said he was expected to work ten to twelve hours a day, then night school, all with a wife and three kids."

"Sounds brutal," Frank said.

"He told me it was killing him," Steven said. "His wife was threatening to leave him and take the kids. His performance at work was suffering, and he didn't have the time needed for the college classes. He tried to do it all and ended up not doing anything very well so he dropped out of night school. Shortly after that, his wife divorced him anyway and took the house and the three kids. With half his assets gone, his 401K looted and a huge monthly child support and alimony payment, Larry was financially and emotionally ruined."

Bobbi's mouth hung open in disbelief, and even Frank's expression turned sympathetic.

"Go on," Frank said.

"Larry admitted to me that he started drinking heavily and spending what little money he had left over at the strip clubs. Needless to say, his work began to suffer. Then the phone company spun off the wireless division and created USA Wireless. One of Larry's old friends offered him a fresh start. He told him if he cut back the drinking and shaped up, he'd bring him over to the new company."

214

"The guy deserved a break." murmured Frank.

"Larry accepted and said he had gotten his drinking under control. His performance at work improved. He met and married his second wife, and things were looking up. He was given the assignment to work with me on the WILCO Project. The project was going great, and he was getting good visibility with senior management. There had been hints that he would finally get his promotion and become the Director of Wireless Game Development when the position was created after the project's completion."

"Wrap it up already, Archer, I gotta crime to solve here," Frank said.

"Alright, alright, I saved the best for last. About six months ago, Larry was emotionally and financially wrecked again when his second wife had an affair with one of his good friends from the phone company. He caught them in the act at his house last Christmas Eve. He left work at eleven to pick her up for a surprise lunch and caught the two doing it in his own bed."

"Jesus, poor guy," Frank said, shaking his head.

"Yeah, he really loved his wife. She left that day, and he was devastated. He started back up with the booze and his attitude and performance at work began to suffer

215

again. The hints of the big promotion stopped and talk of bringing in Jonathan for the director job started."

"How has he been getting along with Jonathan?" Frank asked.

"They tolerate each other, but there is definitely resentment on Larry's part. One night, I think it was in July, Larry invited me to dinner. I think he just needed someone to talk to. He's pretty embarrassed about the second divorce, you know, with his wife having an affair with his good friend and all, so I'm sure he didn't want to discuss it with the guys at work.

"Anyway, we met and he had about eight *Dewars* and waters over the course of the meal. He got wasted. I remember him telling me how he couldn't believe that Jonathan, who is young enough to be his kid, was going to get the job over him. He said he couldn't bear working for someone like Jonathan who was half his age. He pleaded with me to help him with management because he needed the money and he just couldn't stand the humiliation of being passed over again."

"What did you tell him?" Bobbi asked.

"I told him I wasn't really in a position to influence the decision about who was going to get the job. Then he said something that, at the time I thought was the booze

216

talking, but now you need to know. He said, "Mark my words, I'm going to do whatever it takes to get that job."

"Sounds to me like Hershman has a pretty good motive for taking down Jonathan," Frank said.

"He really needs that director job. He definitely has in-depth knowledge of the LBS system," Steven said.

"And you just said he has been accessing the LBS computer, too," Bobbi added.

"That's right. He, Jonathan and Patricia have all accessed the LBS system in the past month."

"So would both Hershman and Patricia have a legitimate reason for accessing that system?" Frank asked.

"Well, yes, except the LBS interface code has been completed for some time and my project plan does not have any further work scheduled on those programs," Steven replied.

"So they might not have a legitimate reason for accessing the computer," Frank said.

"Patricia might be making minor tweaks and not reporting it. That would not be out of the question. And Larry might be working on LBS stuff not involved with our project." Hesitating, Steven sucked in a deep breath. "There's one other thing I think I should mention. This is only a rumor I've heard, so I don't know if it's true or not."

"Let's have it," Frank demanded.

"Apparently, Larry and Patricia are sleeping together," Steven said.

"Interesting." Frank's eyes narrowed. "Maybe they're working together to get Jonathan out of the way. We need to find out more about this love affair. Let's get back to the LBS computer. Why do you think Jonathan's been accessing that system?" Frank asked. "I mean he's a project manager, not a programmer, right?"

"Right, I really can't think of a good reason," Steven replied.

"Bingo. When was the last time Mr. Holden accessed the LBS computer?" Frank asked.

"Looks like Friday." Steven shook his head, feeling guilty for answering Frank's question.

"Bingo, again. Seems pretty interesting to me that our boy, who has no good reason to be accessing the LBS computer, just happens to get on the day before his ex-fiancée is murdered. Tell me honestly, Steven, if Jonathan wasn't working on programs for the project, why would he be accessing that system?"

"The only theory I have, as farfetched as it might seem, is maybe Jonathan suspected that Patricia was sabotaging the project. Maybe he was onto something she was doing to manipulate the location data and was trying to find evidence to nail her."

"Wouldn't he have told you about his suspicions, especially given the rivalry between the two?" Frank asked.

"Jonathan is very sensitive about anything having to do with Patricia. She has been so volatile lately. To be honest, we sometimes think she might be trying to provoke Jonathan so she can come back later and sue for discrimination. I could definitely see Jonathan keeping something like that to himself until he found concrete evidence."

"Wait a minute. You told me yesterday you didn't think that Patricia was capable of sabotaging the game."

"Look, I'm not saying she is, I'm just telling you that is the only potential reason I can think of for Jonathan to be accessing the LBS server recently."

"Or maybe he's hacking the LBS system so he can kill young girls," Frank shot back in disgust. "Did either of you know this Amanda Harvey?"

Both Steven and Bobbi shook their heads.

"I've got a really weird feeling about this case," Frank said, scratching his forehead. "Jonathan's ex-fiancée is strangled. Jonathan has fresh scratches on his face, neck and arms. The killing occurs during the game, which apparently both the victim and Jonathan are playing. It looks like someone has been manipulating the E911 data to facilitate the killing. Jonathan, who has no good or official reason, has been accessing a computer, which is the source of the manipulated E911 location data. Then we find the whole scenario repeated the following night. It almost seems too easy."

"Almost like a frame job," Bobbi chimed in.

"Yeah," Frank said. "Or the killer might have gotten sloppy this time. It looks like we might have recovered some hair and semen evidence from this body."

Chapter Twenty-One

Sunday, November 9 -- 1:41 P.M.

Steven strode back to the *Porsche*, mind numb. Based on the details of the second crime scene, it appeared a serial killer definitely roamed the campus.

Thank God, Jenny is at the beach house.

Steven gritted his teeth and shook his head. Both victims had been playing the WILCO Project game, and it appeared that someone had somehow manipulated the location data resulting from the 911 calls made by the victims from both crime scenes. Hands trembling, Steven struggled to insert the key into the car's ignition.

This is all my fault. Tears welled in his eyes. *How could this have happened on one of my projects?*

He twisted the ignition key, firing up the sports car's powerful engine. Just a few years ago, he had been recognized as one of the world's foremost experts in the computer security field. Disheartened at the thought of tarnishing his legacy as an innovator and leader in his field, he jammed the car into gear and pulled onto the street. Was he to be remembered as a failed college professor whose project was responsible for the deaths of several college students? Steven desperately needed to catch the killer or risk tarnishing his professional reputation.

Dodging the news vans and the crowds of gawking onlookers, Steven passed the second crime scene. As much as he wanted to deny it, circumstantial evidence pointed toward Jonathan as the prime suspect in these killings. There seemed to be two key differences between the first murder and the second. One was the relationship between Jonathan and the victims. The first victim had an obvious relationship with Jonathan, she being his ex-fiancée. Steven had never heard of the second victim. If Jonathan had been dating her or had some relationship with her, surely he would have told Steven about it.

The other difference surrounded the presence of hair and semen evidence at the second crime scene. Why would the killer have been so careful the first time not to leave tracks and so reckless the second time? Did the semen found on the body mean the killer had raped the victim? Frank had never mentioned rape, but that did not rule it out.

Steven powered the *Porsche* around the interstate's banked cloverleaf onramp and aimed his car back toward the beach house. Centrifugal force plastered him against the driver's side door as he pressed the accelerator pedal harder, testing the sports car's formidable handling capability.

Realizing too many questions without any answers overwhelmed him, he reminded himself he needed to focus his efforts on explaining how the E911 location data had been manipulated. With the police watching her, Jenny would be safe at the beach house. Without thinking, he jerked the wheel, crossing three lanes of traffic, barely making the nearest exit ramp, and raced back toward his townhouse just off campus.

Steven entered his residence and made a beeline to kitchen.

I need caffeine, he thought and yanked opened the fridge and grabbed a *Diet Pepsi.*   Reaching into the pantry, he snatched a protein bar, ripped open the wrapper and chomped off a piece and then bounded down the hall to his home office.

If the E911 location data reported to the emergency operator at the PSAP had been incorrect, then the location data sent to the game server must have been incorrect as well. The LBS server at USA Wireless that Peter had logged into the previous day was the source of the location data.

Finishing the energy bar, Steven sat at his desk and then logged into his PC. He clicked on an icon that started up his VPN, or Virtual Private Network, client program. A small login window appeared enabling him to securely connect to the WILCO Project development subnet on the university's campus wide network. He typed his login ID into the VPN window, then entered his password, and in less than a second, the VPN connection completed, securely connecting him into the WILCO Project LAN on the university's network.

Steven logged into a server running the Oracle database that stored information on all the WILCO Project game players. Using first name and last name as keys, he queried the database for Christina Howard's record. Within seconds, Christina's full database record displayed on his screen. He had full privileges for this database giving him the ability to view all of the information stored in the database for Christina, including the user name and password Christina had chosen when she signed up to play the game. He jotted them down on a sticky note and then minimized the database session window.

Steven then clicked on the Internet Explorer icon to start up a web browser. He typed in the URL for the WILCO Project's external website. The site's smart, colorful graphics painted in the display area of the browser. He smiled, proud of the great work the team had done.

He moved the mouse to the sign-in area of the web page located on the left side of the page, just under the top banner. He entered Christina's user name and password in the appropriate fields and then clicked on the "go" button.

He was now logged into the site as Christina Howard. A message popped up in the area where the login fields had previous been displayed that read, "Welcome back, KittyKat!" Moving the mouse over the navigation menu along the top of the page, Steven clicked on the "replay" button.

The mouse cursor showed an hourglass while the *Java* replay program downloaded into the browser. In a few seconds, the download completed, and the replay screen displayed in the browser. Steven clicked on a drop down box listing a series of file names that each included a date and time stamp. The files represented games the user had recently played. He selected the file for the game that Christina had played on Friday night.

Once the replay file finished loading, Steven clicked the "start" button. The screen repainted with map lines and several blue and red icons. The red icons represented members of Christina's team, and the blue icons represented members of the opposing team.

The bottom of the screen displayed a panel that included a series of VCR buttons used to control the speed of the game playback. The bottom panel also displayed a pair of buttons used to zoom in and out, for varying the map's level of detail. The top right of the map contained two digital clocks. One represented the elapsed game time, and the other showed the actual time of day.

On the bottom panel, Steven found a drop down box labeled "View". He clicked on it selecting the "Player" view. This changed the display so the red icon representing Christina moved to the map's center. A small text label corresponding to Christina's user name, "KittyKat," displayed next to the centered red icon.

Steven clicked the play button to start the game replay. The various icons began to make slight movements on the map, except for the KittyKat icon, which stayed perfectly centered. Both clocks advanced at normal speed. The map lines around the KittyKat icon began to move slowly indicating that Christina had begun walking.

Steven clicked the fast forward button several times to increase the game replay speed up to twenty times faster than normal. At 20X speed, the icons and map lines flew around the screen while the KittyKat icon stayed perfectly centered. With the mouse pointer hovering over the "Pause" button, Steven kept his eye on the game clock in the corner of the display. When the clock representing actual time approached midnight, he slowed the replay speed down to double time.

Steven concentrated on the map surrounding the KittyKat icon. Realizing that Christina had begun approaching the intramural softball field, he slowed the replay to normal speed. As the KittyKat icon moved toward the murder scene in the woods behind the softball field's center field fence, Steven noticed a blue icon approaching from a perpendicular angle.

Steven's mouth became dry. He clicked the "Pause" button, took a swallow of his soda, and wiped the sweat from his forehead.

"Holy shit," murmured Steven, realizing the blue icon on the screen represented the killer. Christina's icon headed toward the murder scene in the woods unaware that her killer silently stalked her. Then the blue icon converged on her from a perpendicular angle on a path through the large oak trees, opposite the outfield fence.

A sudden chill snaked down Steven's spine as he realized the killer had somehow used the WILCO Project to hunt down its prey. Steven's stomach soured, and his head spun. He had to figure out the real identity of the player represented on the game replay. That person was the campus killer.

Chapter Twenty-Two

Sunday, November 9 -- 2:28 P.M.

Bobbi Cline skipped up the stairs of the computer center, headed for Professor Archer's office, desperate to talk to him about the campus murders. "Damn it!" she muttered under her breath when found his office door closed. She knocked loudly, but got no response. Placing her ear to the door, Bobbi listened intently for any audible sign he might be behind the closed door, just not answering her knock—nothing.

She snooped around the rest of the offices and cubicles and did not notice anyone around. Continuing her search, Bobbi moved down a hallway and found the computer room. Looking through the plate glass window, she spotted a dumpy looking guy with thick-framed glasses and bad skin. He had a wild mop of black curly hair. Thick sideburns extended down his pimply cheeks to his earlobes, and they were decidedly not neat.

He sat in a chair staring intently at a huge computer monitor. She would not characterize him as obese, but he was bigger than what her mother might describe as "husky". He wore a faded, black concert tee shirt that looked a size too small for his pudgy body. The shirt stretched tightly over his belly and side meat, pulling up in the rear and exposing his lower back and an inch or two of butt crack. His lower half squeezed into a pair of filthy, faded jeans.

Bobbi rapped loudly on the thick glass. Leaning forward, typing steadily on his keyboard, his stare never left the giant monitor. She pounded on the glass as hard as she could with the palm of her open hand, and this time he glanced up at her with an annoyed expression. His eyes locked on her face and then moved down her body. When his gaze slowly moved back to her eyes, he smiled at Bobbi. After that once over, she felt like she needed a shower.

He jumped out of his chair, his pants hanging on to his hips for dear life and walked to the computer room door. Swallowing hard, Bobbi put a sweet smile on her face and the heavy computer room door swung open.

"Hi, I'm looking for Professor Archer. Do you know where I might find him?" Bobbi asked.

"I haven't seen him today. Did you check his office?"

"Yeah, the door was closed, and he didn't answer my knocks. I'm Bobbi Cline." She nearly extended her hand to him but instead crossed her arms over her chest.

"I'm Peter Vaughn. Is there something I can help you with?"

"Do you work here?" she laughed, trying hard to be charming. "Well of course you do, I just saw you working on that big computer in there. What do you do?"

"My official job title is Systems Administrator, but I'm pretty much involved in everything that goes on around here." He turned back toward the computer room and gestured with his hand across the entire room, pointing at all the computer equipment in a single motion. "I operate and maintain all of these computers and the networking gear in those racks way in the back. I am also involved in database administration and security, too," he bragged.

"Wow, sounds impressive. Are you part of the WILCO Project game development?"

A dark expression clouded his face. The question must have hit a nerve.

"Not yet, but I should be. I'm an excellent programmer, better than most of those jerks. I'll be running that development team some day."

"Really. That's awesome, but isn't Jonathan Holden running the project? I saw him speak at the orientation meeting yesterday."

"Yeah, that's him. He's the Project Manager, for now anyway."

"Rumor has it he's going to get a six figure job with USA Wireless because of this project."

"Yeah, but not if that lesbo bitch Patricia has her way."

"Who's Patricia?"

"Jonathan was picked over Patricia Hunter to be project leader and run the development team. Patricia thinks the only reason he got the job is because he's a guy. Man, she treats him like shit, and she's doing everything she can to ruin him so she can take over the project and get that sweet gig with USA Wireless."

"You're kidding."

"Nope." Crossing his arms over his chest, Peter offered her a smile. "So you went to the meeting yesterday? I was there, you know. I kind of head up the game demonstrations and sign up process."

"Cool. Yeah, I was there. I don't think I saw you, but there were lots of people at the meeting."

"We must not have run into each other because I wouldn't have forgotten a pretty girl like you." Peter straightened his glasses and gave her what seemed like his best smile. Bobbi forced a return smile. "So did you play the game yet?"

"Oh yeah, last night. What a rush, I had no idea it would be so intense." She was thankful the conversation had moved in a different direction. "Anyway, I really need to speak to Professor Archer."

"Like I said, I haven't seen him. What do you need? Maybe I can help."

"I wanted to ask him a few questions. I need to get more details about the game."

"More details, how come?"

"I am a reporter for the school newspaper, and I'm doing research for a story I'm writing about the game."

"Really?" Peter's face lit up. "I could help you out, you know, since Archer isn't around."

"But I thought you said you weren't part of the development team."

Peter's happy expression turned wounded, as if he were embarrassed.

"I'm the guy you want to talk to because I manage all the development, testing and production servers for the project. I handle networking, databases and security. I know the details on the game, and I also see the big picture."

"Well, I—"

"Look, I'm not going to hurt you." The smile returned to his face. "Come on into my office for a few minutes."

Holding the computer room door open for her, he motioned her into the computer room. As she stepped into the chilly room, the roar of the heavy-duty air conditioning and hundreds of cooling fans embedded in the computers and communication equipment surprised her. No wonder Peter had barely heard her knocks on the door.

Cold air hit Bobbi from huge ducts in the ceiling. He led her across the raised floor toward his work area. The raised floor consisted of a series of heavy tiles measuring about two feet by two feet. Certain tiles, about every third one or so, had tiny holes in them causing frigid air to blast her from the floor she as passed over them. Goose flesh instantly covered her bare arms and she hugged herself to keep warm.

Peter wheeled a second chair over to his work area for her. She sat down, catching him staring at her chest. Once seated in the chair, she self-consciously crossed her arms over her breasts, hiding his view of her nipples, hardened by the room's chilly temperature.

The guy is creepy.

As much as she wanted to bolt from the frigid room and into the warm sunshine, she resisted and pulled her trusty notebook from the back pocket of her jeans.

"Go ahead, ask me anything you want. It's Peter Vaughn, V-A-U-G-H-N."

"Okay, so how does the game know where all the players are?"

Smiling, Peter launched into a lecture explaining to her about location-based services and how the WILCO Project used them.

Chapter Twenty-Three

Sunday, November 9 -- 2:42 P.M.

Steven stared at his computer screen, the replay of Friday night's game still paused. The red icon, labeled KittyKat, stood ready to continue its approach to the area where workers had discovered Christina's body on Saturday. The blue icon, which he assumed to be the killer, lurked in the woods, daring him to click the "Play" button to continue the game replay. Heart pounding, the sweat from his palm dampening the top of the mouse, he gathered courage to continue.

Before beginning again, Steven noted that the game clock in the upper right hand corner of the screen showed the time at that point in the game replay to be thirteen minutes past midnight. Taking a deep breath, he centered the mouse pointer over the "Play" button and clicked to restart the game replay.

KittyKat slowly tracked to the predicted spot in the woods behind the softball field's center field fence. Steven watched as the blue icon descended on KittyKat's red icon and the two icons intermingled for a couple of minutes.

Steven clapped his hand to his forehead as horror took over. He knew he had just witnessed Christina's virtual murder. He quickly clicked the "Pause" button, freezing the game replay. He clutched his stomach and swallowed hard.

Protein bars don't go bad, do they?

Nausea overwhelmed him, and he retched. Bolting from the chair, he ran to the bathroom to vomit. He emptied the meager contents of his stomach into the toilet and then endured another thirty seconds of painful dry heaves. Stomach settled, he pushed away from the porcelain bowl and leaned back against the bathroom wall.

Tears filling his eyes, his vision blurred. He cried, not specifically to mourn the loss of Christina Howard whom he had known fairly well or Amanda Harvey whom he had never met, he cried because of the overwhelming tragedy of the situation. Some monster had used his game to brutalize these young girls.

How could I have let this happen?

Chest heaving, he sobbed, letting the combined feelings of grief, guilt, anger and fear violently escape him, previously held hostage for the past day and a half. He sobbed hard until his gut hurt, and tears soaked his face.

Physically drained and emotionally purged, Steven reached above his head, grabbed a towel and mopped his face dry. He pictured his beautiful niece, Jenny, and uttered aloud the most sincere prayer he had ever prayed in his life, "Thank you, Lord, for keeping Jenny safe. Thank you."

Feeling a burst of energy and a renewed sense of purpose, he washed his face, brushed his teeth and walked back to his PC.

He positioned the mouse pointer over the "Play" button and clicked the mouse to restart the game playback, observing the red and blue icons still clustered together. Suddenly, the screen went blank except for the red KittyKat icon, which stayed perfectly centered on the screen.

Steven stopped the playback and clicked the "rewind" button to view the game replay in reverse motion. After a couple of seconds, the map reappeared, and the blue icon showed up again. He stopped the playback and switched the view from the player view to the stationary view. In this view, the map location stayed constant so he would always be watching the current spot on the map, which remained the scene of the murder.

He started the playback again, this time in forward motion, and just as he suspected, the red and blue icons mingled together for several seconds. Suddenly, the red icon vanished, leaving the blue icon at the murder scene by itself.

Steven stopped the game playback and minimized the browser window. He restored the window he had used previously to query the game player's database. Querying again, this time using Amanda Harvey as the key, he retrieved the second victim's information. He recorded her user name and password on his sticky note. Finished with the database for the moment, he minimized the window again.

He opened up the Web browser window and clicked on the logoff button to end his session as Christina Howard. The website thanked KittyKat for visiting and encouraged her to visit the site again soon. He clicked on the link provided to return to the WILCO Project home page.

Next, he logged back into the website, this time using the user name and password he had just retrieved from the database for Amanda Harvey. He loaded the game replay for Saturday night and started the playback, this time tracking Amanda's icon, labeled "BadGirl02."

He analyzed the game replay and observed the exact same behavior he had seen when reviewing Christina's game replay. The killer had somehow lured the victim to the spot of the killing and then suddenly they disappeared from the map, leaving only the killer's icon.

Both victims' icons vanishing from their respective murder scenes proved that the same location data had been sent to both the PSAP and the WILCO Project game server. In both cases, location data corresponding to the victims' phones had mysteriously jumped from the actual locations to bogus locations miles away. It was highly improbable that the location data anomalies had been the result of a bug in the LBS software since it had happened exactly the same way in both murder cases and seemingly only at the times of the killings.

**

Sitting on the edge of his bed, Jonathan Holden yawned and stretched his back. Despite getting several hours of sleep, he still felt exhausted. Late night weekend game testing, plus long hours in the office during the workweek had begun taking a toll on him both physically and emotionally. Sunday was his day to catch up on sleep, tend to household chores and pay the bills.

He snatched his cell phone off its charging cradle and pressed the power switch, turning it on. The phone indicated several missed calls and voicemail messages. Deciding to deal with the voicemails later, he walked over to the computer and connected to the university network.

He opened his email and began browsing through the dozen or so new message headers that had arrived in his electronic inbox. Almost immediately, he spotted a message with a timestamp indicating it had been sent earlier that morning from Patricia Hunter. The subject line in the header read, "URGENT: Please respond immediately."

What the hell did she want now?

He clicked on the message header and the body of the email displayed:

Jonathan,

You are going down like a turd flushed down the toilet. I knew you would eventually let your massive ego and your tiny dick ruin you. I hope you like to take it in the ass as much as you like to dish it out, because when your bunkmates in prison get a hold of you, you are never going to want to sit down again!

Here is the best part, I am going to get the job at USA Wireless you stole from me while you get to play the penitentiary version of The Newlywed Game.

Hugs and kisses from your replacement,
Patricia

Jonathan's face reddened and the vein throbbed prominently on his forehead. Clicking the print button he roared, "You bitch!"

Chapter Twenty-Four

Sunday, November 9 -- 3:03 P.M.

Other than the vomiting incident, Steven had not left the chair in front of his computer for nearly two hours. After replaying both murders, he knew the next logical step in his investigation would be finding the identity of the person represented by the blue icon. Continuing along the logic path, taking into consideration everything he had learned about the cases so far, he felt certain the blue icon belonged to Jonathan.

He stared blankly at the computer screen for several minutes, long enough for the screen saver program to kick in. He would much rather watch the university mascot bouncing around the screen than to confirm his awful suspicion that the blue icon represented Jonathan.

For the third time, he queried the game player database, this time retrieving the user name and password for Jonathan Holden. When the information popped onto the screen, he chuckled aloud.

How appropriate, he thought as he stared at Jonathan's user name, "GameGod."

Following the exact same steps as before, Steven used the user name and password from the player's database to log into the website as Jonathan Holden. Pulse quickening, he clicked the "replay" button and loaded the replay application into the browser. Beads of perspiration formed on his brow as he prepared for the final step in his quest to see if killer's blue icon represented Jonathan.

Adrenaline pumping, he moved the mouse pointer over the drop down box and clicked to retrieve the list of replay files. Steven's mouth dropped open in astonishment. When he clicked on the box, no replay files showed on the screen. Blinking his eyes several times, he clicked on the file selection box and again the list appeared empty, indicating no replay files were available for selection.

Impossible, something is wrong!

He had just been using the replay files from Friday and Saturday night's games for the past couple of hours, first signed in as Christina, then as Amanda. The only way those files would not be available to Jonathan was if he had not participated in those games. Steven knew, however, that Jonathan had played the game on Friday because he had told him about it when they met for lunch on Saturday. It was during Friday night's game that the thorny vines in the woods had allegedly scratched Jonathan's face, neck and arms.

The computer stored a single replay file after each WILCO Project game. Steven thrust his hands in the air.

It's the same damn file I just looked at. What the fuck?

He clicked on the refresh button at the top of the browser, forcing the webpage to reload from the web server and the replay application to download again. He clicked on the drop down box and again, the list displayed no replay files. Steven slammed his fist on the desk.

What the hell is going on here?

He logged out of the website, terminating his session as GameGod. Referencing his sticky note, he logged back in to the site as KittyKat and clicked on the "replay" button. After the replay program downloaded, he clicked on the drop down box looking for Friday night's replay file.

Same damn thing!

No replay files listed. Chewing his lower lip, Steven shook his head in frustration. For some reason the system no longer listed any replay files available for viewing. Bolting from the chair, he sprinted for the door, grabbing his keys from the kitchen counter. Steven left the townhouse, his face flushed deep red and headed to the university computer center to figure out why the replay files had suddenly vanished from the system.

He jumped into the *Porsche* and tore out of the parking lot, leaving burned rubber on the pavement. Stomach knotting from nerves again, he contemplated why the replay files might now be missing. It could not have been a hardware failure because if the system had crashed, he would not have been able to load the replay application into the browser.

Bizarre!

Shaking his head, Steven admitted that it was almost as if someone had been watching him work, and as soon as he had been about to identify the blue icon as Jonathan, the files had disappeared. Could Jonathan have wiped the files from the system because he knew they could prove he was the killer?

Steven ripped through the streets unable to get to the computer center fast enough.

***

246

Jonathan Holden reread the email from Patricia for the umpteenth time. He slammed his fist on the computer desk.

That bitch has some nerve!

Why would she send him an email like that? She wanted to provoke him, he concluded. She wanted him to get mad and lose his temper. Jonathan forced himself to take several deep breaths.

Rage subsiding, he reread the email. He rubbed his fatigued eyes. Patricia had clearly threatened him, but he could not figure out how she planned to carry out her threat. The message referenced him going to prison.

Nobody, least of all that bitch, is sending me to jail. If anyone is going to prison, it's going to be her.

By sending him a threatening email, she had left an electronic trail. Jonathan smiled. He had wanted to kick her off the project ever since Professor Archer had picked him over her to be the project leader. This email presented a perfect opportunity for him to get rid of her once and for all.

What a pain in the ass!

He admitted she had performed brilliantly as a software developer on his team. So, for the good of the project, he had put up with her personal attacks. Lately, however, she had gotten out of control. She had crossed the line several times, and it had become harder for him to overlook her verbal attacks and insubordination. This threatening email had gone too far. Patricia had become more of a liability than an asset.

She is so stupid and emotional!

Pulling a stunt like this with the project so close to completion showed Jonathan that she had let her emotions overrule good sense. She had already completed her main contribution to the project, the LBS interface, and it worked like a charm. Consequently, he did not really need her as a developer anymore.

So, why should I put up with her crap? I'll just get rid of her.

Plenty of other students were capable and wanted to finish out the project. Since the tough stuff had been completed already, he could get rid of her and bring in anyone to mop up, even Peter Vaughn.

Patricia was no dummy. She must have known he could and would fire her in a heartbeat after receiving the threatening email. No, she had simply been taunting him. Jonathan's face blazed bright red again.

She's just pissed that I, a man God forbid, beat her out the project leader job. She is a true blue Femi-Nazi.

She wanted to punish him for it! She knew he would get the USA Wireless job, so maybe she figured she had nothing to lose and decided to really stick it to him.

Hell, she probably wants me to fire her so she can try to sue the University for sexual discrimination, he reasoned.

She should have thought about that before she sent this threatening email.

Dumb bitch.

The vein in Jonathan's forehead made an encore appearance.

There is no way I am letting her get away with threatening me. I'll wring her neck!

He picked up the phone and dialed her cell phone number.

"This better be important," Patricia answered.

"What the fuck was that email about? You've got some nerve threatening me."

"What?"

"You know, you're not as bright as I thought you were because this time you left a trail."

"I don't know what you're talking about, Jonathan. I never sent you a threatening email."

"You can deny it all you want, but I have it right in front of me."

"Jona—," she tried to cut him off, but he was on a roll.

"You've been making my life miserable since the day I took over this project. I don't like you and you don't like me, but I never thought you would resort to this kind of unprofessional behavior. I do *not* respond well to threats and taunting. You've gone too far, Patricia, and I'm going to get you thrown off the project."

"Why you—"

Smiling, and with great satisfaction, Jonathan hung up the phone.

Chapter Twenty-Five

Sunday, November 9 -- 3:34 P.M.

Steven slammed on the brakes, screeching to a stop in front of the computer center. He sprinted directly up to Jonathan's office, expecting to find him secretly typing away behind a locked door, deleting files to cover his tracks. Twisting the knob, he found the door locked as predicted. He pounded on the door, but Jonathan did not answer. He quickly checked around and found the remaining offices deserted.

Scratching his head, he jogged down the hall to the computer room and looked through the plate glass window. He saw Peter Vaughn and the student reporter, Bobbi Cline, staring intently at something on Peter's giant computer screen.

Steven slid his university ID through the card reader located beside the computer room door. When a loud click signaled that the bolt in the latch had released, he stepped into the noisy room. He scanned the area looking for Jonathan. Shaking his head, he walked over to Peter's work area. Peter pointed to his oversized computer monitor while explaining something to Bobbi, who nodded back at him. They had not noticed Steven standing behind them.

"Hey Peter, have you seen Jonathan?" Steven asked.

Peter and Bobbi both flinched, surprised by Steven's voice.

"Oh, Professor Archer. I didn't hear you come in. No, I haven't seen anyone all day." Peter looked at Bobbi and smiled. "Allow me to introduce—"

"Actually, we already know each other." Steven nodded to Bobbi after cutting Peter off in mid-sentence. "Hello again, Bobbi."

Peter's expression soured. He obviously had been looking forward to introducing his new female friend.

"Peter, I was looking at some game replays this afternoon when all the replay files just disappeared from the system."

Peter's eyebrows tilted down and the corners of his mouth formed a slight frown, an expression he usually donned when pondering a problem. "What game replays were you looking at?" he asked.

"The replay files for Friday and Saturday nights' games."

"You didn't play in those games, did you? Only players with a user name and password that participated in the games can use the replay function." The intense look on Peter's face showed his mind cranking at full throttle.

"I was showing my niece's friend, who played in the test-games on Friday and Saturday, how the replay function works," Steven lied.

Peter's expression softened. "Yeah, we had a slight problem with the backups last night. Not sure exactly why they failed. I think it might have been a bad cartridge in the tape library." Peter's gaze shifted to Bobbi, no doubt looking to see if he had impressed her with his knowledge of the room's vast array of sophisticated computer equipment.

"Anyway, a little while ago I had to dismount the file system that stores all the replay files and run a check on it to make sure the data was stable. The replay files are okay and should be back on line and available now."

"Thanks." Steven breathed a sigh of relief. That explained why the replay files had suddenly disappeared. He laughed at himself for dreaming up the paranoid theory that Jonathan had secretly destroyed the incriminating replay files to cover his tracks.

Steven turned to head to his office. He paused and looked back to Peter and Bobbi.

"Peter, she really shouldn't be in here. You know the rules."

Peter's gaze dropped to the floor, but before he could reply, Steven hurried down the hall to his office.

***

Shivering from the constant blasts of cold air, Bobbi hugged herself, trying to keep warm. She could not understand how Peter could sit in this icebox for hours on end, wearing only a threadbare, short sleeve tee shirt. She concluded it must have something to do with the extra layer of insulation he had managed to put on his body, probably a result of a constant intake of pizza, junk food and high calorie soft drinks combined with little exercise.

"Peter, thanks for explaining the LBS stuff and how it works with the game. That really helps me out." She glanced at her watch. "Shoot, it's after three-thirty, I really have to go."

Bobbi stood to leave.

"Wait," said Peter with a hint of desperation in his tone. Bobbi's alarm went off again. She had a feeling he was about to hit on her. "I was wondering if, you know, if you weren't busy, I thought maybe we could, you know, get some food later."

Boys are so predictable.

"That's very sweet of you to offer, but I can't."

Despite the frigid air, Peter's face became a deep red, almost a purple color, and she swore a few small beads of sweat appeared on his forehead. He did not like her answer. She could not tell if his expression was a look of embarrassment or anger. She felt a little guilty for crushing him, but for some reason, the urge to run out of the building as fast as she could returned.

She looked directly at Peter. His expression turned normal again, as if someone had flipped a switch somewhere in his brain.

"That's cool. A pretty girl like you probably has a boyfriend, right?"

"No, no boyfriend." The answer slipped out of her mouth before she could stop it. A slight smile formed on Peter's face.

Stupid, she chastised herself, *you left the door open for him.*

"Thanks again for the help. I gotta go." Turning away from him, she took a step toward the door.

"Wait," he called to her. "Let me at least walk you out."

Before Bobbi could react, with the speed and grace of an NFL lineman, Peter jumped out of his seat, sidestepped her chair and stood next to her. They walked out of the freezing computer room, into the warm hallway.

"Peter, I really appreciate your help today."

"No sweat," he replied. Bobbi walked down the hall toward the office area with Peter beside her. "I'm happy to help, anytime, really."

Approaching the end of the short hallway, they heard voices.

"Sounds like someone's here," Bobbi said.

"Yeah, doesn't surprise me. The developers work on Sunday all the time." After exiting the short hallway, they entered the main room with cubicles and offices. The voices came from an open door on the far side on the room. They heard laughing and jovial conversation.

"They must be having a design meeting in the small conference room," Peter said, pointing toward the open door.

"Well I'll see you around, thanks," Bobbi said, ready for the warm Florida sunshine to knock the remaining chill from her body.

"Wait," Peter said again. "If you really want to learn more about the game, you should play again."

"Oh I plan to."

"No, you should play tonight." A huge smile covered his face.

"I didn't think there was a game scheduled for tonight."

"There's not, not for the public anyway. But the project team has a standing game on Sunday nights, real small. The developers usually test out new features they think might go into a future version of the game. It's a closed game, but I might be able to get you in."

"Gee, I don't know."

"Look, you said you wanted to learn about the game, right? I'm offering you a chance to play with the developers. It's a rare opportunity to be part of an internal game where you'll see future stuff that might eventually be added to the game. What more could a reporter want?"

Peter made a lot of sense. This could be an excellent opportunity to figure out how the killer might be using the game, too.

257

A fresh set of goose bumps covered her arms, this time caused by fear rather than the cold air. At the crime scene earlier that day, Detective Diaz indicated that he considered Jonathan Holden the prime suspect in the killings.

"Who all participates in these private games? Does Jonathan Holden play?" she asked, trying to sound casual.

"Jonathan never plays on Sunday nights anymore. He used to, but he's a big shot now." Peter used the two finger quoting gesture as he said, "big shot". "The other players vary, it's usually just a handful of programmers that have something specific to test."

"The game is tonight?"

"Yeah. Wait here, let me check with the guys in the conference room to make sure it's cool."

Peter hurried toward the conference room. Playing in the small private developer's game might be a good idea. Knowing what she knew about the investigation, she probably would not play if Jonathan planned to participate. She considered herself brave, but not stupid. Playing with Jonathan would be too dangerous, but since he did not normally play in the Sunday private games, she felt pretty sure she would be safe.

Besides, I'm a big girl and can take care of myself.

Peter and a young woman emerged from the conference room and walked toward Bobbi. The tall, thick-set woman wore a gray tee shirt under a black warm-up suit with cross trainer shoes. As she and Peter approached, Bobbi could not help thinking that they might make a suitable couple.

"I'm Patricia Hunter." Offering Bobbi a warm smile, she extended her large, almost manly hand. They shook and Bobbi returned the smile.

Dang she's got a strong grip.

"Hi, I'm Bobbi Cline. Nice to meet you."

"Peter tells me you're a reporter doing a story on the WILCO Project?"

"Yes, I am. I write for the school newspaper."

Patricia smiled broadly, obviously elated about the prospect of Bobbi doing the article on the game project.

"Excellent! I want to personally invite you to play in our internal test-game tonight. Have you played the game yet?"

"Yes, I played last night and had a great time."

"Last night's test-game had a bunch of players. You should play with us tonight because there are only going to be a few of us. We're testing out a new upgrade spot the team is considering adding to the game in the next release.

259

A small game has a completely different feel from a large one. It might be something you could contrast in your article."

"Sure, sounds great. Count me in." Despite her concerns about safety, she could hardly turn Patricia down after she asked so nicely.

"Good, I look forward to seeing you tonight. Peter will give you the specifics. I've got to run back into this meeting. It was great meeting you." Extending her hand again, Patricia gave Bobbi another crushing handshake and another big smile and then hurried back to the conference room.

"She is so sweet. Is that the same Patricia you said was out to get Jonathan?" Bobbi asked Peter.

"That's her. She was sweet to you because she wants you to write a great story about the game. She wants to ruin Jonathan, trust me."

"Wow, that's hard to believe, she just seems so...so nice."

"I'm so glad you're going to play with us tonight. Hey, you want to grab some dinner before the game?"

"I really can't."

"It wouldn't be, you know, like a date or anything. It's just that we both gotta eat, and I could give you some more information about the game, you know, for your article."

"I appreciate the offer, Peter, I really do, but I just can't. I've got some other things I have to get done. I'm sure you understand."

"Yeah, I understand," Peter mumbled. The tips of his ears turned red and a half-angry, half-embarrassed expression flitted over his face.

"What time does the game start?"

"Around eight or so."

"Do we meet at the auditorium like last night?"

Peter's mood switch flipped again, and he smiled at Bobbi. "Let's meet at that internet café just off campus at seven-thirty. We can have a drink before the game." Bobbi hesitated before answering. "Look, that's where we all meet before the Sunday night game, and the others will be there too, okay?"

"Sure, Peter, and thanks again for all your help."

"See you tonight." Smiling from ear to ear, Peter headed back down the hall to the computer room.

Chapter Twenty-Six

Sunday, November 9 -- 3:37 P.M.

Steven unlocked the door to his office, still feeling a little silly about his theory that Jonathan had deleted the missing game replay files. He slipped through the door, eager to verify the availability of the replay files Peter had said he had placed back on line. He had to check the replay files for Friday and Saturday nights' games to determine if the player represented by the blue icon was indeed Jonathan Holden. Adrenaline charging back into his system, he quickly closed the office door and sat in front of his computer.

Steven noticed the red message light on his phone blinking, indicating he had a voicemail waiting for retrieval. Who would be leaving him a message at his office on a Sunday afternoon? His stomach turned queasy, and he realized it might be an invitation back to Dr. Herbert's office for another threatening lecture. He picked

262

up the phone and pushed the button next to the red light to retrieve the message.

"Archer, this is Dean Herbert calling. I received another call from the president this morning. He told me about the second body that was found on campus. He also indicated the second victim was playing your game when she died. Let me be clear, Archer. If your game has in any way caused these unfortunate incidents, the project will be canceled. I must also inform you I am considering disciplinary action, including possible termination, against you in this matter. I want to see you in my office first thing Monday morning."

Steven slammed the receiver back on its cradle.

Damn that pompous ass!

The dean had made it his personal mission to force Steven out the university, and there was little he could do to save himself.

Steven buried his head in his hands and took a deep breath. Maybe Dr. Herbert had been right. Perhaps the blame for the deaths of the two girls should rest on him since his game seemed to have played a pivotal part in the murders. Stomach churning, he considered life without his teaching job. He received a great deal of personal satisfaction from teaching. The kids loved his depth of knowledge and real-world perspective. He already had more than enough money in the bank to last the rest of his life so giving young students the benefit of his vast experience had become his passion. He could think of no job he would rather have, he did not want to give up teaching. With no time to waste, Steven refocused on the task of finding the campus killer. He had until Monday, or his job was toast.

He logged onto the WILCO Project development LAN. Pulling the sticky note from his pocket, he signed into the site as Christina Howard. He clicked on the "replay" button, which downloaded and started the replay application in the browser. Clicking on the "Replay Files" selection drop down box, he looked for the game replay files that had previously vanished. Just as Peter had promised, a list of game replay files filled the list box, including the file for Friday night.

Steven started the game replay and watched Friday night's game at high speed. The replay looked exactly as it had when he viewed it at the townhouse. It ended with Christina's icon disappearing, leaving the mysterious blue icon alone at the murder scene. Satisfied, he logged off as Christina Howard.

Steven logged back into the website as Amanda Harvey. He viewed the game replay at high speed. This time, however, when he got to the end of the game replay, he noticed something slightly different from what he observed when he had watched it at home.

He rewound the game replay to the spot where the red and blue icons began to converge on each other. He clicked the "Play" button and watched again at normal speed. The blue icon appeared to be approaching the red icon on a slightly different path.

How is that possible?

Just to be sure his eyes were not deceiving him, he rewound the game replay again. He moved the mouse pointer over the "Play" button. Just before he clicked the mouse button to watch the replay again, he heard a knock on his door.

"Professor Archer, it's Bobbi Cline," a muffled voice called from outside his closed office door.

"Come in," Steven called.

Bobbi opened the door and stuck her head in. "I hate to bug you, I know you are busy."

Steven motioned her into the office. "Please shut the door behind you," he told her. She entered the office and then pulled the door closed.

"What are you working on?"

Steve briefly explained the replay function and what he had observed so far. She moved next to him so she could better see his computer screen.

"So who is BadGirl02?" she asked, pointing at the labeled red icon displayed in the center of his screen.

"That's Amanda Harvey."

"Does that mean this player"—she pointed to the blue icon—"is the killer?"

"That's my theory, watch."

He clicked on the "Play" button, and they watched as the blue icon and the red icon moved toward each other.

"What's that gold thing?" Bobbi asked, pointing to a smaller icon on the screen. "It looks like they're both going to that spot."

Steven clicked the "Pause" button and the screen froze.

"Huh? Yeah, I was so focused on the two players I hadn't really noticed that before. You've played the game, right?"

Bobbi nodded her head.

"That icon represents the location of an upgrade spot."

"Oh right, so these players are racing to that spot to grab the upgrade."

"That's what it looks like."

"Did you notice the same thing on Friday night's game?"

"Now that you mention it, I'm pretty sure there was one."

Steven clicked the "Play" button to continue the game replay. They watched as the red and blue icons came together. Bobbi's hand moved to her mouth, which hung open.

"Oh my God, he's killing her, isn't he?"

Steven did not reply. Suddenly, the red icon vanished. He looked at Bobbi, whose complexion had turned a pasty white.

"Are you okay?" he asked her.

She swallowed hard. "Yeah, I'm all right." She drew in a deep breath and after exhaling through pursed lips, asked, "So who is the blue icon? How come it doesn't have a label like the red one?"

"It actually does have a label, we just can't see it because of privacy issues. We only label the icon of the player signed into the website and running the replay function."

"Okay, so right now you must be signed in as Amanda because she's BadGirl02."

"That's right."

"Don't you have some program that could play back the games with the labels of all the players' icons displayed?"

Steven laughed. "That would be nice, wouldn't it." He shook his head. "No, the development team was working on something like that to use as a tool for verifying the accuracy of the LBS location data, but we stopped working on it because the location data has been so pinpoint accurate. We've never finished it because there were other, more important features we needed to add to the game."

"So the only way to find the identity of the killer is to log into the website as each player on the blue team that played that night, one at a time and track their movement."

"Yes, but given what we know about the case so far, I think it's obvious who we should try first."

"Jonathan Holden," Bobbi replied, eyes wide.

Steven halted the current game replay and signed out of the website as Amanda. He clicked the link and returned to the main page so he could sign back in as Jonathan. He typed Jonathan Holden's user name and password into the proper boxes and clicked the "Go" button.

The website displayed the message, "Welcome back, GameGod," verifying Steven had successfully signed in as Jonathan. He started up the game replay application and loaded up the file for Friday night's game.

Steven positioned the mouse pointer over the "Play" button. He and Bobbi looked at each other, realizing they were on the verge of potentially identifying the person responsible for killing two young women on campus.

Giving her a nod, he clicked the mouse and game replay began. He clicked the fast forward button several times to accelerate the replay speed. They watched the icons and map lines whirl around the black background, focusing intently on the clock in the screen's upper right hand corner. The clock approached midnight, and Steven slowed the replay down to normal speed. Steven and Bobbi watched in horror as GameGod, also known as Jonathan Holden, moved directly toward the exact spot in the woods, behind the centerfield fence of the intramural softball field where his ex-fiancée, Christina Howard, had been brutally strangled.

Chapter Twenty-Seven

Sunday, November 9 -- 4:14 P.M.

Covering his face with both hands, Steven leaned back in his chair, unable to comprehend what he had just witnessed.

How could Jonathan be a cold blooded killer?

Despite all the evidence indicating that he committed the murders, Steven never truly believed Jonathan could be the campus killer. He could no longer deny it now. He and Bobbi had just witnessed Jonathan digitally murder Christina.

"Professor Archer, are you okay?" Bobbi asked.

Steven scrubbed his face with his hands. "Yeah, I just didn't think Jonathan was the one, you know?"

"Yeah, I guess you guys were pretty close, working together and all."

"We were, we definitely were close." Pulling his hands from his face, Steven looked at Bobbi and slowly shook his head. "Just to be thorough, I want to run the replay for Saturday night's game."

"Good idea."

Steven signed into the website as Amanda Harvey. He loaded up Saturday night's game replay file. They watched the game replay together, a digital movie with the same ending, just a different victim killed in a different spot.

Some of this horror story had begun to make sense to Steven. Jonathan must have lured the victims to the isolated places on campus and then committed the murders. The bait, as Bobbi had pointed out earlier, must have been the upgrade spots. Jonathan could have hacked the game so only his intended victim could "see" the upgrade spot, thus setting a trap for her.

Jonathan must have also hacked the LBS system to alter the location data for an incoming 911 call from the victim's phone. That would explain his frequent sessions on the LBS server over the past month or so.

Steven sighed, thankful his earlier attempts to contact Jonathan had failed. He very well could have tipped him off, allowing him to cover his tracks or flee the country. Frank had been right, and Steven felt guilty for doubting him.

This case was not over yet. They had identified Jonathan as the killer, but he was still at large. Swallowing hard, he grabbed the phone and dialed the beach house. After several rings, Jenny answered the phone.

"Jenny, it's me."

"Hi, Uncle Steven."

"Is everything alright?" he asked, trying to sound calm.

"Sure, we're locked in here just hanging out."

"Good. Listen, we are pretty sure the killer is Jonathan Holden, so do not, under any circumstances, let him or anyone else in that house, okay?"

"Jonathan's the killer, are you sure?"

"That's what it looks like, I'll explain it all later, but I've really got to go."

"Okay. Goodb—"

"Wait, Jenny, don't tell the others just yet, and nobody comes in the house."

"Okay, don't worry."

They hung up.

Taking a deep breath, Steven dialed Frank's cell phone. He picked up almost immediately.

"Steven, what's up?"

"It's Jonathan."

"Hold on. What do you mean?"

"Jonathan Holden is the killer," Steven barked, his heart racing.

"Slow down and take a breath. How do you know for sure it's Jonathan?"

Steven took several breaths and then explained what he and Bobbi had just witnessed on the game replays.

"Stay right where you are, I'm coming to your office. I'm at the second crime scene so I'll be there in just a few minutes."

Hanging up the phone, Steven turned to Bobbi.

"Frank is on his way. He wants to see the game replays."

Steven rubbed his eyes, ready to wake up from this horrific nightmare. The police just needed to catch Jonathan before he hurt anyone else.

"It's hard for me to picture Jonathan Holden as a killer. He is so handsome and well spoken. I was very impressed with his presentation yesterday."

"He's quite a—"

Suddenly, the office door crashed open, and Jonathan Holden burst into the office.

Bobbi let out an ear-piercing scream. Bolting from his chair, Steven stood between Jonathan and a cowering Bobbi.

"I'm going to kill that bitch, Patricia," Jonathan yelled, spit flying. His face had turned crimson, and the vein pulsed on his forehead. Nearly hyperventilating, he waved a white sheet of paper toward Steven.

"Have a seat and calm down," Steven ordered, pointing at a chair next to the office door.

Steven put an arm around Bobbi and ushered her to the door, carefully keeping his body between Bobbi and Jonathan.

"You better leave, I'll call you later," he said to Bobbi, letting her out of the office, leaving the door open.

"Jonathan, what the hell is wrong with you?" Steven demanded.

"She's gone too far this time." Standing up, he violently shook the paper. "Look, she threatened me!" He took a step toward Steven. "Read the email she sent me this morning. That fucking bitch." Taking another step forward, he thrust the paper at Steven.

"Freeze!" Without warning, Frank jumped through the office doorway, gun drawn and trained on Jonathan's head. "Put your hands in the air and slowly back away from the professor."

Jonathan's mouth hung open in complete shock. He dropped the paper and immediately put his hands above his head. Slowly, he obeyed the detective and took two tentative steps backward, away from Steven.

"What's going on?" Jonathan asked, turning his head to look at Frank.

"Shut up and keep your eyes forward," Frank said. "You okay, Steven?"

Steven nodded.

Frank cuffed Jonathan's hands behind his back and spun him around, looking him in the eyes for the first time. Jonathan returned the look, eyes wide, his lower lip quivering.

"Jonathan Holden, you are under arrest for the murders of Christina Howard and Amanda Harvey."

Chapter Twenty-Eight

Sunday, November 9 -- 4:37 P.M.

After reading Jonathan his rights, Frank and the other police officers quickly removed him from the computer center and transported him to the city lockup for booking. Jonathan had been extremely cooperative during the arrest. He followed the officers' orders without a struggle. The stunned expression shown when he first saw Frank's gun pointing at his head had never really left his face. He kept insisting repeatedly he was innocent, and that he didn't even know about the murders.

Frank had told Steven he had stormed his office, gun drawn, because he had heard Bobbi's scream as he came up the stairs to see about the game replays. When he got to the office, he couldn't see Bobbi and from his view through the open door, it looked like Jonathan was attacking Steven.

276

Steven, alone in his office, looked out of the window, seeing nothing but Jonathan's baffled expression in his mind. The sound of Jonathan's desperate voice, pleading for help, echoed in his head. Steven occupied the same position he had a day and a half earlier when this nightmare had begun. How could a seemingly perfect weekend turn so tragic in roughly thirty-two hours?

A killer had brutally murdered two college students and his friend and prodigy had just been arrested for killing them. The project he had masterminded had been hacked and abused by Jonathan to isolate and then strangle the girls.

Steven had watched the game replays and witnessed Jonathan stalk his prey, tracking the victims to their final destinations where he killed them in cold blood. Obviously, the police had enough evidence and probable cause to arrest Jonathan.

Despite the overwhelming evidence provided by the replay files, something about the bewildered look in Jonathan's eyes as the police led him away seemed genuine. The look portrayed such surprise and puzzlement, almost total confusion on Jonathan's part.

Don't be fooled, Steven thought.

Jonathan had pulled off a superb acting job. He apparently had been performing since the day they met. How else could Steven have worked so closely with him and not know he was capable of murder? He had been bamboozled by a real psychopath.

Steven heard a knock on his office door. Swiveling his chair, he saw Peter Vaughn sticking his head through the door.

"Peter, come in."

"Professor Archer, are you okay?"

"Yeah, I'm okay, considering. Did you see them take Jonathan away?"

"I just happened to look up and see a cop standing at the end of the hall. When I came out of the computer room to see what was going on the police escorted me outside. I could see they had Jonathan in cuffs. I guess they were reading him his rights or something. God, his expression was...I don't know, he looked stoned or something. Anyway, they told me I could come back up after they got him out of the building and on his way to jail."

"Was anyone else in the office besides you and me?" Steven asked.

"Nope. Patricia and some of the others had a design meeting earlier, but they had just left. The cop told me Jonathan is being arrested for murder. He wouldn't give me any details. What's going on?"

"Peter, I can't really talk about it. There's an investigation, you know.

"Sure, I understand. I'll let you get back to work."

Peter left the office.

Now that the police had arrested the killer, Steven set about discovering how Jonathan had hacked the LBS system at USA wireless. He knew he would need help from Larry Hershman. It was late afternoon on Sunday, the odds were Larry was drunk as a skunk and not much help. If Larry did not pan out, he would have to deal with Patricia Hunter.

Steven tried calling all of Larry's numbers—work, home and mobile. He struck out on each and did not bother leaving messages. Next, he tried calling Patricia's numbers. Same result, no answers. He left urgent messages for her to call him as soon as possible at each number. If the rumors were true, Larry and Patricia might not be able to get to the phone because she had tied up and gagged him, and was busily administering punishment with a riding crop.

Steven spun his chair around to face his computer. Taking a deep breath, he logged into the WILCO Project development server that stored the source programs for the game and began looking for answers as to how Jonathan had committed the crimes.

***

At a quarter after five, Steven's office phone rang. He had been dissecting the WILCO Project game programs for less than an hour, and his head had already begun to throb. He grabbed the phone receiver from its cradle, grateful for the forced break.

"This is Steven."

"Hi, it's Patricia. I just got your message. What's up?"

"Patricia, thanks for calling back. I need your help."

"Sure, what do you need?"

"It's about Jonathan, have you—"

Patricia cut him off. "If this is about some threatening email that he's claiming I sent him, well, I didn't." Her tone was both defensive and agitated.

"Patricia, please, calm down. He did show me an email, but—"

"Calm down? You want me to calm down?" she shouted angrily. "He called me this morning about this so-called threatening email. Well, I never sent him an email. In fact, I never even logged onto email this morning."

"Patricia, listen I—"

"I'm sick and tired of your boy constantly pulling this crap. Just because he's the project leader, he thinks he can get away with accusing me of threatening him with an email. I'm not taking it anymore."

"Hey, Patricia, stop," Steven barked into the receiver. "Please, listen. I don't think you understand."

"Oh, I understand all right. You're going to take his side like you always do. You men always stick together."

Steven threw his free hand into the air in frustration. "Hold on a second. What do you mean? I don't always take his side."

"Yeah, right. Let's face it. You two are pals and just because I'm a woman, I'm on the outside looking in."

"Damn it, Patricia, that's just not true."

"Well that's the way I see it. Just like today, you call me about some email I never sent. You're taking his side."

"First, I didn't call you about the email. Second, I've got the email you sent to Jonathan right in my hand. So don't lecture me about taking sides."

"He's lying. I didn't send any email to Jonathan. This is bullshit. I've got to go, I'll talk to you tomorrow."

"Wait! Patricia, don't hang up."

Too late. Patricia ended the call.

Damn it!

Why did she have to be so difficult? He had not called her to discuss the email Jonathan had received. He had simply wanted to ask if she would help him figure out how Jonathan had managed to manipulate the LBS location data.

Chapter Twenty-Nine

Sunday, November 9 -- 5:32 P.M.

     After completing the booking process, a pair of uniformed officers led Jonathan, hands still cuffed behind his back, into a small interrogation room. The officers seated Jonathan in an unpadded chair with a red plastic bucket-like seat situated on one side of a heavy table. They told him to stay seated and then left him alone in the room.

     He stared at the tabletop in front of him, covered with pen and pencil graffiti and marred with carved initials and innumerable cigarette burns. An identical chair sat on the opposite side of the table. An accumulation of dirt and second-hand smoke had rendered the walls and ceiling of the once white room a pallid yellow color. Jonathan barely recognized his own reflection staring back at him from the large mirrored window build into the wall directly across the table.

After several minutes, the door opened, and Detective Diaz entered the room.

"Are you going to give me any trouble if I take those bracelets off, Jonathan?" Jonathan hesitated, cocked his head slightly at Detective Diaz and shrugged his shoulders. The detective smirked at him, balled his hands up and put his wrists together. "The handcuffs, Jonathan, do you want me to take them off?"

"Yes, please," Jonathan croaked weakly.

The detective produced a tiny key and moving behind Jonathan, removed the cuffs. Keeping a constant eye on him, Detective Diaz positioned himself across the table, directly opposite Jonathan, with his back to the two-way mirror. Pulling the empty chair from under the table, he put his foot up its seat and leaned an elbow on his raised knee.

"Two counts of murder one, Jonathan. Victim number one is your ex-fiancée, Ms. Christina Howard. Victim number two is a freshman student, Ms. Amanda Harvey. Tell me son, how did you get yourself into this mess?"

"Oh God." Jonathan's head dropped, and he rubbed his eyes. "Like I told you before, I am innocent."

"Why should I believe you are innocent?"

"Because I didn't kill anyone. I didn't even know Christina and Amanda," his voice cracked, "were...dead, until you arrested me."

"Jonathan, look at me. Steven, Professor Archer that is, tells me you're a real bright guy. So put yourself in my shoes. Two dead bodies show up on campus. I've got a suspect in custody with a clear motive. His motive is that his fiancée of a year and a half broke up with him a couple of weeks ago. His pride was hurt. He was humiliated. His friends are constantly busting his balls about him getting dumped. He tried hard to get her back, but she is done with him. Maybe she called him to pick up her toothbrush or perfume or whatever else she may have left behind. Maybe they argued again. Maybe my suspect tried to convince her they should get back together, but she shot him down again."

"No," Jonathan tried to protest.

"Shut up and listen. Now everyone knows that my suspect has a huge ego and an even bigger temper. Maybe my suspect, the golden boy who always gets what he wants, couldn't have Christina. So he figured a way to show Christina who's boss. If he can't have her, nobody's going to have her. That's a pretty good motive, right Jonathan?"

"No, I didn't—"

285

"There's more to the story, so follow me, Jonathan. My suspect had been with his fiancée for a year and a half. She's a real looker, and he's gotten pretty used to a steady diet of pussy. He gets dumped and after a couple of weeks is starved for some physical attention. He's major league horny. So my suspect picks up a beautiful freshman babe to satisfy his needs. This girl is smokin' hot, see, but Amanda is young and likes to fool around. Maybe she won't go all the way. My suspect is used to getting what he wants. He doesn't like some bimbo to get him all hard then not finish the job. So maybe he got a little rough with her. Maybe he forced her to have sex. Afterward he realized what he had done and that big Fortune 500 wireless companies don't hire rapists, he fixed the situation. And why not, it was easy, just like the night before. How's that for a motive?"

"But I—"

"Shut up, Jonathan. Let's talk about opportunity. Both my victims were lured to isolated places on campus to meet their demise. Both just happened to be playing a new cell phone game that is the latest craze on campus. Now it just so happens that my suspect is running the development project for this popular game. Because of the game replay technology, we have a record of my suspect at the scene of the murders with the victims at the time of their death. That gives my suspect opportunity to commit the crimes."

"That's impossible, I—"

"Finally, the murder weapon. Both victims were strangled by the killer's bare hands. Hold up your hands Jonathan."

Jonathan stared blankly at the detective, not moving.

"Hold your fucking hands up, now," Detective Diaz roared.

Jonathan slowly raised his hands off the table, a fearful expression on his face.

"I can plainly see that my suspect has both of his hands. Put your goddamned hands down." Jonathan lowered his hands. "You see, Jonathan, just like in the movies I have motive, opportunity and the murder weapon. Hell, I got more than that. You were observed with fresh scratches on your face and neck only hours after the first killing. But where we are really going to nail you is the DNA that you left in Amanda. Once we get those lab results back, this case will be closed."

Chapter Thirty

Sunday, November 9 -- 6:51 P.M.

Steven had remained in his campus office poring over countless programs, looking for any clues as to how Jonathan had used the WILCO Project to commit his crimes. So far, he had found nothing, and frustration and fatigue had begun exacting their toll on him. His office phone rang, and he ripped the handset from the base unit. He answered the phone to find Frank on the other end of the line.

"Steven, I've got a problem."

"What's going on?"

"We've been questioning Jonathan Holden for an hour and a half, and he denies any involvement in the murders. Hell, he swears he didn't even know about the murders until we arrested him in your office."

"Does that surprise you?"

"It didn't at first. Just about every suspect we question in that interrogation room is innocent. Shoplifters to murders to rapists—seems none of them have ever committed the crime."

"So what's the story with Jonathan?"

"We've made him tell his story over and over again, looking for him to slip up, you know, mix up a detail or something. His story is exactly the same each time. He says he played the game Friday night. Got scratched running into some thorny vines in the woods. Went home alone after the game early on Saturday morning. Got up and gave a presentation at the auditorium on the game. Met Amanda Harvey after the meeting when she signed up to play the game. Made plans to see her in his office that afternoon to tutor her on the game. Had lunch with you and Larry Hershman. Met Amanda in the office after that for the game lesson. Went home alone and took a nap. Took Amanda to dinner. They went back to his place and had consensual sex. They left his place and met the other players at the auditorium to play the game. They split up when the game started, and that was the last time he saw her. After the game was over, he went straight home and slept until three in the afternoon today. He got up and checked his email. That's when he read the threatening email from Patricia. He got pissed and went to your office to talk to you about it. That's when we arrested him."

"That can't be true, I mean I saw where he, or at least his phone, was at each murder scene with each of the victims. Did he have his phone when you arrested him?"

"He did. I also asked him if his phone had been out of his possession at any time since Friday, or if he had lost it or misplaced it. He swears his phone was in his possession at all times."

"He has to be lying."

"There's more. We talked with the owner of the restaurant Jonathan claims to have taken Amanda Harvey to last night. A Mr. Giglio confirmed they did have dinner at his place, and he spoke to Jonathan and met Amanda. There were several other employees that verified his story."

"But Frank, just because he took her out to dinner doesn't mean he didn't kill her later."

"I know that, but let me finish. I checked with the medical examiner, and she said the evidence doesn't clearly show Amanda was raped. She definitely had sex last night, but the ME doesn't think it was rape."

"Again, that still doesn't mean he didn't kill her later."

"Look, I'm just saying Jonathan's story makes sense. I couldn't trip him up. He consistently gave me the exact same details, and these other facts we've checked up on are suggesting he's telling the truth. The other thing I'm having a problem with is my own intuition."

"What do mean?"

"In my gut I don't think he did it."

"What? What about the scratches and the game replay?"

"I just spent an hour and a half with this kid, and I don't think he killed those girls. First, he might be one hell of an actor, but he was emotionally destroyed over the deaths of both. I mean, once it actually hit him that those two were really dead, he was a mess. First, he became very emotional, you know crying his eyes out and then he sort of zoned out. He was answering questions and all, but he was definitely in shock, not all there."

"He could be putting on a show for you."

"Sure he could, but the other thing bugging me is his motive for killing Amanda. I mean I could see the revenge motive for Christina dumping him, no problem. But if he and Amanda were all snuggly at the restaurant and then she willingly had sex with him at his apartment, then why did he kill her? My original theory was that he might have raped her and possibly killed her to try and cover that up. But she had sex with him willingly. Plus, he's too smart to leave DNA on the body, he knows that would come back to haunt him."

"I see what you mean, maybe he lost his temper and things went too far and he ended up killing her."

"I just don't see that. I mean if he lost his temper during an argument, he wouldn't have lured her to the construction site and then stalked her while playing a game to kill her. If he lost his temper then he would have strangled her wherever the altercation took place and at that time."

"I see your point. He's got no apparent motive for killing Amanda. So did you ask him about the LBS location data being off and the game replay putting him at both crime scenes?"

"Yeah, and he had no idea how that could have happened. He said there are only two people that could've pulled that off, Larry Hershman or Patricia Hunter. He said he was being framed by Patricia because she is jealous of him and wants his job."

"Patricia has made his life hell since he took over the project."

"Do you think she could be setting Jonathan up?"

"She did write the LBS interface, so if anyone is capable of hacking the LBS system it's her. To pull this off she would have had to hack both the USA Wireless software and the WILCO Project software."

"Didn't you tell me she is one of the people you found out was accessing the LBS computer?"

"Yes, and she could have been accessing that computer to modify the USA Wireless system that feeds cell phone location data to both the E-911 system and the game. She would have also had to hack the game server at the university to make her icon look like Jonathan's. She also probably somehow modified the game so the upgrade spots that lured both victims to those remote locations were only visible to her and the victims."

"Can you try to check that out for me?"

"I'm already looking."

"Thanks. The other thing Jonathan kept talking about was this email Patricia supposedly sent him this morning. He said in it, she threatened him with prison."

"Yeah, it's very strange. Jonathan brought me a printout of the email, let me read it to you."

Steven read the email to Frank.

"Sounds to me like she wants Jonathan out of the picture. You think that email is really from Patricia?"

"I'm not sure. I find it very hard to believe she would send something like this to Jonathan. I mean, she's too smart to leave an incriminating trail like that. But—"

"But what, Steven?"

"Well, it's just that she has really been acting aggressive lately, more aggressive than usual. There was her altercation with Jonathan Saturday morning at the game presentation where she baited Jonathan and got him to lose his temper."

"What else?"

"After you guys took Jonathan away, I had a short phone conversation with her. I tried to ask her if she could help me figure out how Jonathan might have manipulated the LBS data."

"What do mean *tried*?"

"When I tried to ask her if she had heard about Jonathan's arrest she cut me off because she thought I was calling her on the carpet about the email."

"So she defended the email?"

"No, she denied sending it. I kept trying to tell her I didn't care about the email, but before I could get through to her she hung up on me."

"That's strange."

"Yeah, very weird. It's almost like she was over-sensitive about the email, like she was denying it way too hard."

"I'm going to send someone to question her."

"Remember, if that rumor about her is true, she might be hanging out at Larry Hershman's apartment."

"Right."

"What are you going to do about Jonathan?"

"We're going to hold him. His dad has hired some hotshot lawyer who is on the way. My gut tells me the kid is innocent, but there is no way I would cut him loose. The prosecutor would have my job. We don't have any solid evidence other than the game replays. If this lawyer is as good as they say, we might not have enough on Jonathan to keep him in custody anyway."

Chapter Thirty-One

Sunday, November 9 -- 6:54 P.M.

After ending the phone call with Frank, Steven stood and stretched his aching back. The conversation had overwhelmed him and he needed a break. Grabbing spare change from his top desk drawer, he left the office and headed for the vending machines on the first floor lobby.

Steven had never wanted to believe Jonathan had killed the girls. He now felt a measure of satisfaction that Frank somewhat shared his opinion. He did not kid himself about Jonathan's innocence or that this nightmare was over by any means. Too many questions remained.

If Patricia had committed the crimes and framed Jonathan, how had she known about him and Amanda? According to Frank, Steven had met Amanda for the first time Saturday morning at the game presentation while she signed up to play. Patricia had been there as well, working one of the sign-up tables. She must have noticed and maybe even overheard the conversation when the two met and agreed to see each other later that afternoon in his office.

Could Patricia have picked Amanda as the second victim based on that encounter? It probably depended on how Jonathan and Amanda had interacted. Perhaps they had overtly flirted with each other making it obvious they were strongly attracted to one another. That might have been all she needed to see to mark Amanda as the next victim in Jonathan's framing.

But what about the threatening email? Steven scratched his head. *Why would she leave an incriminating trail like that? Maybe she intended to go back into the mail server and erase the original message and then claim Jonathan had simply created the message himself to try and throw off the authorities. In fact, evidence of the email might have already been removed from the email server.* He made a mental note to check on that.

Patricia's new romance with Larry Hershman also nagged at him. In order to hack the LBS system to manipulate the location data, she might have needed some help or cooperation from someone at USA Wireless. Larry had been assigned as the team's LBS expert. He was where she would go for LBS assistance.

The LBS software providing location data for cell phones on the network executed on a server owned and operated by USA Wireless in their data center. Patricia would not have the ability to directly access that server or the LBS software. Larry, however, would have access to that system. Maybe Patricia had used her relationship with Larry to get his account name and password to hack into the LBS software system.

She could have altered programs in the LBS system to watch for 911 calls from a particular cellular number. When the 911 call came into the LBS system from that specific number, she could have bypassed the normal processing and forced the location data to point to a certain location. Larry might be an accessory to these crimes and not even know it.

Larry had a motive to set Jonathan up as well. He would have known about Jonathan's breakup with Christina. Everyone associated with the project knew about that. But he was not at the orientation meeting when Jonathan met Amanda. How would he have known about the budding romance between Jonathan and Amanda?

Jonathan could have easily said something to Larry when they had met for lunch on Saturday. Steven had left them alone together for several minutes when he had talked

298

to Frank in the back of the restaurant. Knowing Jonathan, he had probably bragged to Larry about this hot new girl he had met that morning and how he was going to see her after lunch. Could hearing Jonathan brag about snagging a beautiful freshman girl when his own wife had cheated on him with a friend and then left him in financial ruin be enough to push Larry over the edge and target Amanda as the next victim?

All of these theories swarmed in Steven's brain as he returned to his office, determined to find some clue buried in source code of the WILCO Project that would identify the campus killer.

***

At just after seven-thirty, Bobbi Cline entered *Hot Java!,* an internet café located a couple of blocks off campus. She had found it in a shabby strip mall, sandwiched between a discount hair salon and a mortgage broker specializing in clients with "less than perfect credit."

The café combined a coffeehouse with a beer bar and featured a limited snack bar menu, the antithesis of those Seattle-type franchises with nine-dollar cups of coffee and designer pastries. Instead of clean, comfortable couches and elegant wrought iron table and chair sets, the owners had furnished the joint with a group of mismatched garage sale sofas and rickety second-hand tables and chairs. The room smelled like burned grease and stale beer. Dust bunnies and grit congregated on the floor in the room's crannies, and dirt seemed to cling to the furniture's worn upholstery.

On the left side of the room two ancient, twelve-foot rectangular banquet tables had been place side-by-side with their long edges pushed together. Each table had five PCs configured so the monitors faced out, away from the center of the tables. Beyond the tables a Formica countertop with a couple of mounted beer taps and a few odd bar stools sitting in front served as the bar.

Behind the bar, a serve-through window had been built into the back wall that looked into a small kitchen with a fry vat and a greasy grill. A short man with a huge belly covered by a dirty, once-white apron slouched on a barstool behind the makeshift bar, reading a tabloid and chewing an unlit cigar.

Bobbi looked to the right side of the room and spotted Peter sitting in one of the threadbare couches situated on the back wall with a laptop computer balanced across his knees. He had a beer in one hand and beckoned to her with the other.

"Hi!" Peter stood and placed the open laptop on the couch where he had been sitting. He offered her a big smile.

"Hi, where is everyone else?"

"They'll be here soon." He straightened his glasses. "What do you think? Cool place?"

"Yeah, this is not what I expected. What's with all those computers over there?" Bobbi asked, pointing to the group of computers on the other side of the room.

"Those are for multiplayer games. See, they're on their own one hundred gigabit switched LAN, so there's like no network latency." Bobbi nodded her head but had no idea what Peter had just said. "This place rocks on Friday and Saturday night with gamers. They have tournaments and stuff. I know the owners. They're buddies of mine from school."

"There's no one in here. How does this place stay open?"

"It's always slow on Sunday nights. They get a decent coffee crowd in the mornings and during the day, mostly students who can't afford Starbucks. They serve burgers and sandwiches for lunch and dinner. They also sell beer. Speaking of which, can I get you one?" Peter drained the remaining half of his beer from the red plastic kegger cup.

"No thanks."

"I'm getting myself one, it's no trouble. Come on, my treat."

"No thanks, I'm fine."

"Have a seat, I want to show you something when I get back." He pointed to a spot on the couch next to where his laptop rested.

Bobbi sat on the ancient couch, sinking so low that her knees ended up higher than her hips. She thought she saw a cloud of dust rise from the couch as she sat.

Where the hell are Patricia and the rest of the group?

Peter returned and plopped down beside her on the couch, placing the laptop back on his knees. He angled the PC toward her so she could view the screen.

"I thought you might want to see how we set up a WILCO Project game. I'm going to set up tonight's game so you can watch."

"Sounds great."

This might be good.

If she had to sit next to the guy, she might as well learn more about the game.

Peter opened a browser and typed in the address for the WILCO Project website. He-signed in and clicked on the "Create Game" button located on the navigation bar at the top of the page. A map displayed in the body of the browser with the university computer center located in the middle.

"First thing we want to do is define how big we want the game area to be. The center of the game defaults to the university computer center, which is the center point on our map. We could change the center point to anywhere in the USA Wireless coverage area, but we are going to leave it alone. Remember that the game area is like the court in a basketball game. You have to stay on the court or you are ruled out of bounds. Same thing in this game, if the computer detects that you have left the game area, you are automatically eliminated from the game."

"I understand," Bobbi said.

"Good. In our case, we left the center point as the university computer center. So, all we have to do to define the size of the game area is specify the radius of the circle. The game area will be calculated from the center point. So, if I make the radius three miles, the game area will be a big circle that is six miles across with the center at the university computer center. Understand?"

"Sure," she answered. "So, if I start at the computer center and walk in a straight line in any direction for three miles, I will be at the edge of the game area."

"That's right."

"If I continue on that line beyond three miles I will be kicked out of the game."

"You got it. One thing to remember is, if you think you are close to the edge of the game area, just look at the radar on your phone. The out of bounds is displayed in a solid gray color. As long as you don't cross into the gray, you are fine. I am going to go ahead and make the game area for tonight have a three-mile radius."

He entered the number in the proper field in the browser. "The next thing we do is specify what types of upgrade spots there are and how many we want. I think we are going to have about six players tonight, so I'll put eight upgrade spots out there for us to find. I'm going to let the computer randomly choose which type of upgrade spots to deploy and also randomly place them on the playing area. I am also going to specify that two of those upgrade spots should be the new ones that the team wants to test tonight."

He entered the information into the browser. "Now we specify what type of game to play. Tonight it will be every man for himself, or a game of sole survivor."

"So the last player standing wins, right?" Bobbi asked.

"Right. Next we pick a start time and make this a private game." He specified eight-thirty p.m. in the start time field. He clicked a check box labeled "Private Game" and typed in a game name, "SunTest," and a password "EvisR8."

"This is the same game name and password we use every Sunday night. That's all there is to it." He clicked the "Done" button at the bottom of the screen.

"Now that the game is created, we just have to sign up to play in the game." He clicked on the "Play!" button on the top navigation bar.

A short list of game names appeared in a drop down box. He selected the "SunTest" game and typed in the correct password. A message confirming he was now signed up for the game with a reminder that the game would begin at eight-thirty appeared on the browser.

"Now I will sign out of the website so you can get into the game." He clicked the "Logoff" button and handed the laptop over to her. "Just type in your user name and password to sign into the website and then click the play button and do what I did."

Bobbi followed his directions and within thirty seconds, she had signed up to play in the test-game. She looked at her watch and noticed it was almost eight o'clock already.

"Where are the others? I thought you said they were going to meet us here." She tried hard to keep her apprehension from displaying in her voice and expression.

Peter gulped down his beer. "Relax, here they are now."

Bobbi looked at the door and saw Patricia, an older man and two other students enter the café and head toward them. She smiled, relieved that the rest of the group had finally joined them.

Bobbi guessed the older man had to be Larry Hershman. He stood taller than she had expected, about six feet even, she estimated. He had a slight build except for his prominent beer belly. His arms and legs were skinny and he had no visible rear end. Short gray hair covered the top of his head. The expression on his nondescript face made Bobbi think he would probably rather be doing something else that night.

All the players except Bobbi had dressed about the same. They wore dark tee shirts, jeans and athletic shoes. Bobbi also wore jeans and athletic shoes, but she hadn't thought to change out of the pink, short sleeved, button down blouse she had put on that morning.

So much for hiding in dark alleys.

Patricia arrived at the couch first with her man-like hand extended, smiling warmly.

"Bobbi, I am so glad you could join us tonight. You're going to have a great time. Let me introduce Larry Hershman, a project manager from USA Wireless. Larry's been working closely with us on the WILCO Project. Larry, this is Bobbi Cline. She's the reporter I was telling you about that's doing the story on the WILCO Project."

"Nice to meet you," he mumbled, giving her a limp handshake, then turned and made an immediate beeline for the bar.

"Our other two players are Darryl Summers and Milan Gupta. They are student developers on the WILCO Project." Patricia pointed at the remaining two students. Darryl and Milan had clustered around Peter's laptop, busily signing up for the game.

"Did Peter show you the game set-up process?" Patricia asked.

"Yes, he did. It was really very interesting. Thanks Peter." Bobbi threw Peter a bone since he really had done a great job of demonstrating how to set up a WILCO Project game. She glanced over at Peter and, just as she had predicted, saw he sported a massive grin—the smile, so genuine and puppy-like, almost made him tolerable.

"It's after eight, so we better get going and split up. Any questions, Bobbi?"

"No."

"Okay, remember your phone will beep at eight twenty-five with a text message telling you to start the game on your phone. At eight-thirty, the game is on."

Bobbi thanked her again for allowing her to participate in their private game and then left the café to get ready for the start of the game.

Chapter Thirty-Two

Sunday, November 9 -- 8:23 P.M.

Steven smiled as he pulled the *Advil* bottle he had finally found from the depths of his desk drawer. Swallowing a couple or three of these modern marvels of medicine, and in about ten minutes, the throbbing pain that had engulfed his skull would magically cease. He ripped off the childproof cap and pulled the seemingly endless wad of cotton from the small plastic bottle's neck. Empty. He swore under his breath and flung the useless bottle at the trashcan near the door.

What kind of moron takes the last tablet, stuffs all the freaking cotton back into the empty bottle and then puts the empty bottle back in the desk drawer?

Nothing had gone right that evening. He had been scouring the WILCO Project programs for hours. He was not sure what he was looking for, and all of the lines of code had begun to look the same. His mind numb and back aching, he tried to relieve his tension by kneading the knots in his lower lumbar with the knuckles on his balled-up hands. Exhausted and hungry, he felt like going home and taking a long hot shower then eating an entire large pizza.

He stood and stretched, then moved from behind his desk and without thinking, did twenty quick jumping jacks. He instantly felt better, not good, but invigorated. He returned to the familiar spot in front of the computer and rubbed his tired eyes.

I have to keep going.

The programs that made up the WILCO Project were kept in a source code library. The library was a tool the team used to ensure that two developers did not work on the same program at the same time. The tool worked just like a digital library. If a developer wanted to work on a program, he or she had to check it out of the library. No one else could work on that same program while it was checked out. When the developer had finished working on the program, he or she checked it back into the library making it available for others again.

The source code library also created a record of who had had checked out what programs and when they did the work. Each time a developer checked a program out of the library, he or she was required to specify their reason for modifying the code. The date and time the program had been checked out and then back in was recorded as well. A report could then be run against the library that chronicled the evolution of the project.

Steven searched the library for LBS interface programs that had been checked out by Jonathan or Patricia over the past few weeks. He had double-checked the project plan and there had been no scheduled modifications to the LBS interface in the previous two-and-a-half months. No one would have had an official reason for modifying any of those LBS interface programs.

Steven found a program that had been checked out by Jonathan a week and a half before. The reason he specified for checking it out read "Update in line documentation."

What was this?

Why would Jonathan be updating the documentation in a program Patricia had created? This anomaly definitely required further investigation.

Steven opened the program in his editor. The large program consisted of several hundred lines of code. He began analyzing the program by first slowly scrolling through the lines of code. Not sure exactly what to look for, he tried to identify how many comments, also called in-line documentation, had been added to the program.

Right in the midst of this scanning process, the lines of code stopped scrolling down his screen for a split second, even though he had not lifted his finger off the keyboard. The hesitation in the scrolling struck him as odd but he continued with his scan. The scrolling hesitated a couple of more times in rapid succession and in one case, the screen froze for at least a half second.

Something weird is happening!

A change in the system environment on the server had caused the scrolling hesitations. Some other program must have started up on the server causing his editor to experience the momentary glitches. This was not necessarily abnormal. Developers compiling code or running systems tests might have caused the brief pauses, or perhaps the nightly backup of the server to tape had kicked in.

Steven opened another window and typed in a command to list all users currently using the server. He rubbed the rough stubble on his chin, only his ID displayed on this list. That meant no other humans had logged on to the server. He ruled out the tape backup job because it was only eight-thirty and the backups were performed at three in the morning.

What the hell was causing the server to bog down?

Steven typed another command that listed the active programs currently running on the system. He immediately recognized that the list contained the WILCO Project game programs. Then it hit him, the hesitations on the server had been caused by someone starting up a WILCO Project game.

***

Bobbi Cline stopped running for a second to catch her breath. She had barely escaped being captured by Patricia by sprinting as hard as she could for several hundred yards. Only her quickness had allowed her to elude Patricia's attack.

Breathing hard with sweat streaming down her face and neck, she took a seat on the edge of a fountain in front of the Humanities building. She hung her head and stared at the pavement near her feet, exhausted from the chase. She suddenly bolted to her feet, after seeing her shadow on the ground. Looking up she realized the overhead streetlight bathed her in bright amber light.   *I'm a sitting duck out here!*

Cursing, she flew toward the corner of the building located about thirty yards away and took up a position on the other side of the building's corner, shaded from the streetlight.

She slumped down with her back against the building to rest her legs. Using the back of her hand, she squeegeed the sweat running from her forehead into her eyes. Squinting in the dim light, she searched beyond the fountain for signs of Patricia, who had probably had a chance to catch up to her by now. She saw no one with her naked eye and pondered using her radar.

Lacking experience with the game, she never quite knew when to use the radar. She desperately wanted to verify she had given Patricia the slip, but she also knew that in doing so, she would be advertising her exact position. If Patricia were out of radar range it would not matter, but if she were close by, the chase would be on again.

Bobbi decided to take a look with the radar. Finding the last dry spot on her sweat-soaked shirttail, she wiped the drops of perspiration from the phone display. Taking a deep breath and focusing on the phone display, she activated the radar.

Damn it!

An enemy icon had appeared on the screen. Patricia must have caught up with her. Bobbi estimated the distance between her and her pursuer to be about one hundred and fifty yards.

At the very edge, on the opposite side of the phone display, she noticed a small gold icon—an upgrade spot. She guessed that the icon represented a cloaking upgrade. Still focused on the display, Bobbi stood to get her bearings. She appeared to be located between Patricia and the upgrade spot. It looked like the upgrade spot was situated at or near the big parking garage just down the street.

Bobbi turned off her radar. Although still a newbie at the game, she recognized an opportunity to turn the tables on her opponent and stop playing defense and start attacking. She planned to lure Patricia to the upgrade spot, but get there first to claim the upgrade. Once invisible to Patricia's radar, she could then execute an ambush and eliminate Patricia from the game. Carefully looking around and seeing no sign of Patricia, Bobbi set off toward the upgrade spot.

Chapter Thirty-Three

Steven typed in the command to list the active programs running on the system again. Something did not look right, but he could not quite figure out what about the list bothered him. He studied the list of currently running programs one more time, and then it jumped off the screen at him.

The main program that executed the entire WILCO Project game was named "mstr-gserver.exe." The program currently running the active game had a slightly different name, "mstr_gserver.exe." The name contained an underscore instead of a hyphen. The subtle difference in the name meant a non-standard version of the game program currently ran on the system. Although he did not have proof, Steven knew in his heart the killer's deadly version of the game now executed on the server, and someone out there playing the WILCO Project game was in grave danger.

***

Bobbi alternated between walking and jogging. She could see the five-story parking garage just a half a block up the street. Every minute or so, she flipped on the radar, monitoring the enemy icon's position behind her. She slowed her pace, allowing her prey to catch up to her. Since this was an individual game, the threat of an ambushed by two opposing teammates, like what had ended her game the previous night, did not concern her.

She approached the parking garage from the side of the building, away from the street. Flipping on the radar, she absorbed the details of the display, and then turned it off. Her enemy had closed in on her now.

The upgrade spot appeared to be in the exact center of the parking garage. She did not have the opportunity to claim an upgrade in the previous night's game, so she did not know how close she needed to get to the icon to activate the upgrade. When she looked back down the street, she saw the outline of a person approaching the garage.

Time to move!

Bobbi glanced in all directions making sure no one watched and climbed up and over the four-foot concrete wall into the ground floor of the dimly lit parking garage.

***

Fingers hammering the keyboard, Steven logged into the database server. He queried the database, searching for the players actively engaged in a WILCO Project game. The resulting list showed six active players. One player's name in the list immediately grabbed his attention. A chill ran down his spine as he blurted out the name, "GameGod!"

Son of a bitch! How can Jonathan be playing in an active WILCO Project game?

As of a few hours ago, he had been locked away in the county jail. Frank told him he had changed his mind and did not believe Jonathan had murdered the girls, but he also remembered Frank saying he planned to detain him as a precaution. Maybe the Holden family's high-powered lawyer had pulled some strings and managed to spring Jonathan from jail. It seemed unlikely, but perhaps political favors had been involved. Regardless, Steven called the station in search of Frank to determine if Jonathan had been released. The officer at the other end of the phone informed Steven he had seen Frank at the station earlier and asked him to hold while he went to track Frank down.

Putting the call on speakerphone, Steven examined the other game names on his list of active players. The next name that jumped out at him was "NewsHound."

Oh, shit!

That had to be Bobbi Cline. He queried the players' database and verified the user name "NewsHound" did indeed belong to Bobbi.

A voice on the speakerphone interrupted the looping on-hold PSA describing the Crime Stoppers hotline.

"Hello?"

"Yes, I'm here."

"We can't seem to locate Detective Diaz. Can I take a message?"

"Yes, can you tell him to call Steven Archer? It's urgent."

"Does he have the number?"

"Yes. Can you please tell me if Jonathan Holden has been released?"

"Sir, it is the department's policy to—"

"Okay, okay." Steven interrupted. "Please have Frank call me."

Without waiting for an answer, Steven slammed the receiver back in its cradle. He scanned Bobbi's database record, which he had left displayed on his screen and found her cell phone number. He dialed the number and without a ring, a click sounded on the line, and a generic voicemail greeting started to play, indicating her phone was most likely set to "Do Not Disturb." Players in an active game typically put their phones in DND mode so incoming calls would not interfere with their game play. When the voicemail greeting ended, he left an urgent message for her to call him as soon as she received his message.

Steven queried the database again, this time searching for the record containing specific information about the game currently being played. The database reported a single active WILCO Project game called "SunTest." He saw the game had been started that night at eight-thirty and marked *Private*, meaning players needed the secret password to join the game.

Steven found the private game password field in the database and grabbed a pen and his pad of sticky notes to jot the password down. As soon as he read the password, he tossed the pen aside because he knew he would not soon forget it. His heart pounded in his chest, and his stomach turned over with fear. The password chosen for the active game was "evisR8," an obvious abbreviation for the word "eviscerate".

Spooked by the menacing password, Steven quickly opened a new web browser window and entered the URL for the WILCO Project website into the browser's address field. Once the page finished loading, he signed into the site using his own user name and password. He clicked on the "Play!" button and selected the "SunTest" game in the list of current games. A chill running through his body, he typed "evisR8" into the password field and clicked the "Join" button.

Steven had entered the "SunTest" game as an active player. He whipped out his cell phone and with fingers flying, punched in a series of symbols and characters on his phone's keypad and hit the send button. A short trumpet sound played out of the phone's speaker and the message "God's Eye Mode" flashed for three seconds on his phone display. When the message stopped flashing, the WILCO Project game map painted on the display with all of the enemy icons and upgrade spots visible.

Steven had enabled a cheat, or secret feature, called "God's Eye Mode". Very few people even knew about this mode because it had only been used in very early test-games. Once the cheat code was transmitted from the phone to the game server, the player gained the ability to view every icon across the entire game area without having to use the radar feature. Players in "God's Eye Mode" did not show up on any other player's radar, so they were invisible.

Using his thumbs on the phone's arrow keys to pan around the map of the game area, Steven quickly found what he was looking for: a blue icon bearing down on a red icon, both headed for a golden upgrade spot icon.

Hoping this situation was not a repeat of what had occurred in the woods behind the softball field and in the partially constructed building, Steven sprinted downstairs to his car.

Chapter Thirty-Four

Sunday, November 9 -- 8:52 P.M.

Bobbi peered back over the side wall of the parking garage she had just scaled, to see if anyone had witnessed her enter the structure. She did not see anyone except the figure of her enemy approaching from up the block. Dirty white lines marked the empty parking spaces located along the length of the outside wall where she crouched.

To her right at the front of the building, an automatic gate and self-serve ticket machine guarded the entrance to the garage. She squinted at the glass cashier's booth located at the garage's exit, on the opposite end of the building to her far left, looking for an attendant. The booth appeared to be unmanned. In the center of the building on the entrance end, she found the bottom of the ramp leading to the second parking level. She noticed that sets of stairs leading to the five parking levels were located in each corner of the structure. To her left, toward the rear of the first floor, under the ramp was a pair of elevator doors.

Bobbi checked her radar. The enemy icon had nearly caught up with her, converging on the front entrance of the garage. Keeping low, she sprinted to the corner stairs at the rear of the building, slipped into the stairwell and quietly ascended to the second level.

Checking her radar again, she saw the enemy had entered the front of the building and now traced her steps on the ground floor, heading toward the stairs she had just climbed. In a few seconds, her foe would be directly below her.

The upgrade icon appeared to be situated in the exact center of the building. In order to claim the upgrade, she would have to sprint down the car ramp that connected the first and second levels.

Hearing footsteps on the stairs below her, Bobbi left the stairwell and shot across the rear end of the garage. She did not look back at the stairwell, fearing her pursuer might have made it up the stairs and was poised to take a face shot at her. When she got to the edge of the ramp, she veered to her right and sprinted down the ramp.

The ramp was steeper than she expected and she misjudged her speed as she completed the tail end of her sharp turn. Her momentum carried her far enough into the empty parking spaces that she planted her foot on a fresh oil spot. Knowing she was about to lose patches of skin on multiple parts of her body she tried to brace for the impact. She could do nothing to prepare for the impending fall other than slam her hand to her face, attempting to keep her glasses from flying off when her body impacted the rough concrete.

For a brief moment, Bobbi's body flew through the air, parallel to the ramp. Then she landed hard on her right hip, sparing her knee. A split second after initial impact, her elbow smashed into the concrete, absorbing the blow and saving her head from bouncing off the ramp. She barrel-rolled three times down the ramp, guarding her face with the arm that hadn't broken her fall.

Somehow, she managed to keep her glasses on her face and avoided dropping the cell phone. Blood oozed from both elbows, but the abrasions were not as bad as she expected. The elbow she landed on had already begun stiffening, but she did not believe it was broken.

She stood and completed a quick check of the rest of her body, only finding a few minor bruises. Straightening her glasses, she took a tentative step, testing her hip. It hurt, but she could still walk. Certain her pursuer would be rounding the corner at the top of the ramp at any second, she limped down the ramp to claim the upgrade.

***

Steven tore out of his parking space at the computer center, heading to the parking garage on the opposite side of the campus. He screeched to a stop at the exit of the computer center parking lot and called Frank's cell phone. Getting no answer, he shouted a message into Frank's voicemail instructing him to meet him at the campus parking garage as soon as possible and to bring help.

***

Bobbi half jogged, half limped, a few more yards down the parking garage ramp, trying desperately to claim the cloaking upgrade. She had progressed almost to the midpoint of the ramp when her phone emitted a series of tones. She stopped and looked at the display. The screen flashed and a message congratulated her on earning the upgrade and informed her that cloaking had been activated.
Cool!

Her radar had been switched on so she could see the enemy, and she knew the enemy's radar could not see her. She noticed a timer in the corner of her phone display that read four minutes and fifty-three seconds. She had less than five minutes of invisible time left.

***

Steven pulled out of the computer center parking lot, smoking the tires on the *Porsche*. He dialed 911 on his cell phone but the line rang and rang. He counted nine rings before the line clicked on.

"Hello, I need help," he yelled into the phone.

"You have reached the nine-one-one emergency response center. Due to unusually heavy call volumes, you will be placed on a short hold. Please do not hang up and call back. Your call will be answered in the order in which it was received."

***

Bobbi stared at the phone display. Her radar showed her enemy trying to trick her by doubling back to the opposite end of the garage. The blue icon was not

327

positioned at the top of the ramp as she had expected, but actually moved toward the other end of the garage along the far side of the building, the side on which she had first entered the structure.

She reversed direction and ran as fast as her stiff and sore hip would allow, past the spot where she had slipped and wiped out, to the top of the ramp on the second level. She stopped and studied the phone display. The blue icon had changed direction and now approached the stairs on her left, the same stairs she had used to go from the ground floor to the second level. She headed for the opposite stairwell on the far side of the structure.

Damn, she thought, *Patricia is pretty good at this game.*

Despite having claimed the upgrade and therefore invisible to any opponent's radar, it appeared to Bobbi that Patricia knew her exact location and was now moving directly toward her.

Phone to eye, ready to snap the picture, she cautiously peeked out of the stairwell, across the end of the garage where Patricia should have been approaching.

No one there!

Her opponent must have gone up to level three.

Damn it!

She ducked back into the stairwell and painfully climbed the stairs to the third level. Looking at her phone display, she noticed the blue icon had progressed halfway across the end of the garage but had also moved thirty feet or so toward the center of the structure.

She peeked out of the stairwell again and traced the route the blue icon had taken since leaving the opposite stairwell. Her gaze stopped in the vicinity of the elevator doors, just on the other side of the ramp.

That was it!

Her opponent knew Bobbi had the upgrade and could see but could not be seen. Patricia must have headed for the elevator hoping the cell signal would not work inside the elevator car. If the signal on her opponent's cell phone did not work, then the blue icon would disappear from Bobbi's display, and in the confusion, her opponent would escape.

Nice try, Patricia.

Bobbi cautiously exited the stairwell. The blue icon still appeared to be waiting by the elevator. She dashed across the garage, past the ramp and flattened herself against the wall of the elevator shaft. If she had figured this out correctly, Patricia should be just around the corner waiting for the elevator car to escape the garage.

Bobbi took one last look at her phone display and verified the blue icon remained positioned just around the corner by the elevator door. She took a deep breath and swung around the corner, finger on the trigger, ready to shoot the picture with her phone.

No one was there. She had prepared herself for this possibility as Patricia could have gone up, one level above her, or possibly down, a level below her. The logical choice for Patricia would be to go down to the ground floor and flee the garage, so Bobbi planned to beat her to the ground floor and catch her when she exited the elevator.

Turning to head back to the stairwell, she caught a glimpse of something sitting on top of the trashcan by the elevator door. She did a double take.

It's a cell phone!

She looked at her phone display and noted that the blue icon occupied the exact same spot on the map as the real cell phone did, right by the elevator door. Realizing something was terribly wrong, Bobbi felt the adrenaline flood her body. Instinctively, she whirled to escape the garage, but before she could take a stride, a powerful hand clamped across her mouth as she was grabbed from behind.

Chapter Thirty-five

Sunday, November 9 -- 9:03 P.M.

Steven felt as if he had been on hold with the 911 call center for several minutes when it had actually been less than thirty seconds. It took him much longer than that to give the operator directions to the campus parking garage because he did not know the exact street address.

He also had a hard time trying to explain to the operator that he had called to report a possible murder in progress at the parking garage. The operator did not believe him and decided to ask him a few qualifying questions. How did he know someone was going to be killed? How did he know the location of the murder would be the parking garage? Was Steven going to be doing the killing? After wasting valuable seconds, he was finally able to convince the operator to send a squad car to the parking garage to check out the situation.

Approaching the parking structure, Steven cut the *Porsche's* headlights and stared at his phone display. To his horror, the red and the blue icons had migrated to the center of the garage and appeared to be stuck together. Hoping he had not arrived too late, he dialed Frank's cell phone again and left him another urgent message to get to the parking garage as soon as possible.

***

Bobbi trembled with fear. She had been gagged with a large bandana pulled so tight across her mouth she felt the urge to heave. A thick black ski cap had been placed on her head and pulled down over her eyes, effectively blindfolding her. She had no idea who had captured her, as her captor had not spoken a word, only uttering an occasional grunt. Her hands had been secured behind her with a large wire tie.

Her captor led her away from the elevator to the corner stairwell. They climbed the stairs to the fourth level. Bobbi considered her options for escape. She could not scream, and she could not see. The wire tie securing her hands had been tightened to the point that it dug into her wrists, and the slightest hand movement caused searing

332

pain. Even if she could break free, the injury to her hip, caused by her earlier tumble down the ramp, had made walking painfully difficult. With each step, her throbbing hip stiffened, and she knew running away from her captor was just not possible.

They exited the stairwell and moved back into the interior of the garage. She felt them descend as they walked so she knew they were moving back down the ramp connecting levels three and four.

After a short walk down the ramp, they halted. Her back exploded in pain as her captor pinned her against a concrete wall. She tried to protest but as soon as she attempted to speak, the powerful hand clamped back across her mouth causing her to gag and making breathing difficult. Bobbi shook her head, indicating she would keep quiet, and her captor pulled the hand away from her mouth.

Her back still pushed against the wall, her tormentor forced her legs together, nearly causing Bobbi to topple over, and bound her ankles with another thick wire tie. As she struggled to maintain her balance, strong hands grasped her shoulders and spun her a half turn. She heard a snip, and to her surprise, the wire tie that had cinched her wrists together behind her back was cut, freeing her hands.

Bobbie drew her arms in front of her and rubbed her right wrist, feeling the deep intentions left by the wire tie. Before she could massage her wrist, her captor grabbed her shoulders again and in a single motion, rotated her body and slammed her back against the wall. Caught off guard, the back of Bobbi's head bounced off the hard concrete and her blank field of vision filled with shooting stars of pain.

As she fought to maintain consciousness, she felt her captor cinch each wrist to thick support cables that ran along the sides of the ramp parallel to the floor. Her captor had attached her wrists to the support cables using wire ties that dug even deeper into her wrists, causing immediate tingles in her fingers.

Bobbi shook her head and sucked air into her lungs through her nose. Her head cleared, and she tried unsuccessfully to move her arms and legs. She stood with her ankles bound tightly and her back pinned against a vertical concrete wall. Her arms had been spread wide, perpendicular to her body, so she resembled the letter "T". Any attempt at movement resulted in searing pain in her bound wrists.

Bobbi felt a hand on the crown of her head. The hand slowly moved over her forehead and down over her nose. Fingers grasped the bottom of the ski cap and the

334

hand ripped the cap off her head allowing Bobbi to see again.

Blinking several times, it took a couple of seconds for Bobbi's eyes to adjust to the presence of light. Eyes wide, trying to scream, Bobbi stared into the face of the campus killer.

Chapter Thirty-Six

Sunday, November 9 -- 9:06 P.M.

Steven jumped out of the *Porsche*, which he had parked on the street in front of the parking garage. He studied his phone display and found the two icons located in the center of the parking garage. He squinted up the street for any sign of the police and seeing nothing, sprinted for the structure.

***

"Hello Bobbi," Peter Vaughn said with a huge grin on his face. "First things first."

He pulled Bobbi's cell phone from his pocket and dialed 9-1-1. He placed the phone to his ear for several seconds then hung up. "Let's just send the cops on a wild goose chase." He laughed.

Peter reached out to Bobbi and unbuttoned the top button of her shirt. Bobbi twisted her shoulder, but the immediate pain caused by the wire ties digging into her wrists forced her to stop struggling. She looked and saw blood dripping from a deep cut caused by the wire tie.

"Bobbi, it's best that you don't struggle. Now where were we?"

Peter undid the remaining buttons and opened her shirt. He stared intently at her nearly naked torso with a glassy expression.

"All you had to do was go on a date with me, Bobbi. We could have avoided all this nastiness."

He stared at her, but his eyes seemed distant, as if he were in some sort of fantasy dream state. He reached out and caressed her breasts over her exposed bra.

"Why are girls always rejecting me, Bobbi? I know I'm just an average-looking guy, but they should look past that and try to get to know me." Peter's expression hardened. "Like you, Bobbi. Would it have been so bad for you to go on one date with me? If you had just tried to get to know me you would have found out I'm a great guy. You would have liked me. You would have wanted to be with me. But you're just like the rest of them, aren't you, Bobbi?"

He ripped the left cup of her bra down, exposing her breast. He pinched her nipple hard, bringing tears to her eyes.

Seeing Bobbi's tears, his expression shifted again. An apologetic look washed over his face. He reached toward her and she flinched, causing the ties to dig deeper into her wrists.

"I'm sorry, I didn't mean to hurt you." He gently pulled her shirt back in place, covering her body. "It's not your fault. It's this fucked-up society. People need to learn that us unpopular smart kids have a lot to offer. People like Jonathan. Jonathan won't give me a chance because I'm a nerd."

Peter's face and ears turned red and his mood swung back to anger. He offered her an evil laugh.

"Well, this nerd is fighting back! Jonathan is going to learn the hard way. He is going to prison for killing Christina and Amanda. He killed those girls. I might have strangled the life out of them, but he forced me to do it. If he had just given me the chance to work on the development team, he would have seen that I'm a great programmer. I wouldn't have had to set him up to get him out of the way. We could have avoided all this nastiness."

Peter ripped her shirt open again and yanked her bra down, exposing her breasts. Bobbi tried to scream and struggle, blood dripping down her forearms from the deep cuts on her wrists. Peter clamped a hand over her gagged mouth and roughly fondled her chest with his other hand.

She continued to struggle, but the wire ties felt like they had cut into the bones of her wrists. Blood streamed down her forearms and dripped off her elbows, splattering the wall and the ramp below.

Feeling lightheaded, she stopped struggling. Peter was mesmerized by her naked chest and leaned his face in toward her breasts. Bobbi saw a slight movement in the shadows on the other side of the ramp. While Peter kissed her chest, Bobbi watched as Professor Archer snuck across the ramp behind Peter.

Peter pulled his head away from Bobbi's body and smiled at her.

"That's not so bad now, is it? Feels good, right?"

Trying to smile through the gag, Bobbi nodded her head, playing along.

Peter bent down and unsnapped her jeans. Professor Archer now stood just a few feet behind Peter holding a tire iron in his hand, an index finger pressed against his lips. Peter fiddled with her zipper.

Eyes wide, her chin quivering, Bobbi made eye contact with Professor Archer while fighting the urge to scream. He slowly shook his head, trying to calm her.

Peter successfully opened the front of her jeans and stood, gawking at Bobbi. "Are you going to be a good girl and let me undo your feet?"

Bobbi nodded her head.

Professor Archer, directly behind Peter now, slowly raised the tire iron above his head. Peter caught Bobbi's gaze darting from his face to somewhere above his head.

Just as Professor Archer swung the tire iron down at Peter's head, Peter spun around and dodged the blow.

Chapter Thirty-Seven

Sunday, November 9 - 9:09 P.M.

Steven swung the tire iron at Peter's head. Spinning to face him, Peter made a slight move to the side and dodged the blow. The tire iron clanked off the concrete ramp, doing little damage. The follow through left Steven bent at the waist and vulnerable. Peter took advantage by pivoting and pushing Steven's hips toward the base of the ramp.

Already off balance from swinging the tire iron, Peter's push forced Steven off his feet. He landed on his back and rolled several times down the ramp, losing the weapon in the process.

Peter grabbed the tire iron with both hands. Smiling, he advanced toward Steven who struggled to his feet.

"Asshole Archer, what a surprise. No one invited you to this party."

Steven tried to sound calm and confident. "Put the tire iron down, Peter. The police will be here any second."

"That's funny, I don't hear any sirens." He laughed. "I wasn't expecting you, but I'm glad you showed up."

Lunging at him, Peter swung the tire iron hard, barely missing Steven's head. Steven side-stepped him and swung his fist as hard as he could, connecting with Peter's ear.

Peter grunted and swung the tire iron wildly at Steven, like a tennis backhand shot, missing completely. The momentum from the swing opened Peter's front to a waiting Steven, and Steven smashed his fist directly into Peter's face.

Peter instantly screamed. Blood streamed from both nostrils, and Steven knew he had just broken his nose. Peter's eyes watered profusely, and his expression showed a look of serious pain.

Steven checked his balance then aimed a kick right at Peter's crotch. To his surprise, the kick landed squarely where he had aimed, right into the testicles. A half-scream, half-gasp escaped Peter as he doubled over, dropping the tire iron.

Steven grabbed the tire iron and faced Peter who looked like he was about to pass out.

"You give up?" Steven yelled, noting a hint of surrender in Peter's expression.

"Fuck you," Peter answered in a raspy sort of squeak, and Steven knew the boy was done fighting.

"Sit down and stay put," Steven commanded and then jabbed the tire iron at Peter's head.

Peter flinched and then sat on the ramp groaning as his rear end hit the concrete.

Steven backed up the ramp toward Bobbi, eyes never leaving Peter, who sat rubbing his lower abdomen and moaning.

Reaching Bobbi, Steven tried to comfort her.

"Bobbi, just relax. The police are on the way."

Bobbi tried to respond, but Steven could not understand her because of the gag.

"It's okay, I'm going to take the gag out of your mouth."

Keeping his gaze on Peter, Steven turned toward Bobbi. He carefully put the tire iron between his legs. Peter still sat on the ground, head down, rocking himself. The groans had turned to quiet whimpers.

Steven allowed himself a quick glance at Bobbi's face, just for a split second. Peter had knotted the gag tightly in the back. Steven knew that in order to remove the

343

gag, he would have to take his eyes off Peter. The knot behind her head was very tight, and he wanted to limit any movement of her body to minimize further damage to her wrists. The only way to accomplish that was to look at the knot while he untied it.

"Bobbi, I'm not sure I can take the gag out."

He stole another look at her face, and she began to sob. Tears streaming down her face, her eyes pleaded for the gag to come out. Steven looked back at Peter who still sat rocking away, nearly comatose.

"I'll try to do this, but you've got to help me. Turn your head and watch Peter. If he starts to get up let me know."

She nodded, turned and stared at Peter, giving Steven better access to the knot. Steven looked away from Peter and covered Bobbi's bare front by closing her shirt.

Concentrating on the tight knot, Steven started to remove the gag. Before he got the first loop undone, Bobbi's eyes widened and she tried to scream. With unbelievable speed, Peter had jumped to his feet and bull-rushed Steven.

Steven could barely pull the tire iron from between his knees before Peter was on him. He wielded the weapon defensively as Peter lunged. Anticipating the move, Peter blocked the weak swing and knocked Steven to the ground. Jumping on top of him, Peter pinned Steven's arm to the concrete with his knee and grabbed the tire iron with both hands. With barely a struggle, Peter ripped the weapon from Steven's hand.

He had pinned Steven with his full body weight rendering him helpless. He tried in vain to buck Peter off while Peter just laughed. Running out of strength, Steven's attempts at escape became weaker.

"You underestimated me again, Archer. You thought you had me whipped over there, but I outsmarted you. I've always known I was smarter than you. Now I'm gonna punish you, asshole."

Peter raised the tire iron above his head, the sharp, flat end pointing down at Steven's chest. Sweat dripping off his chin, Peter's face twisted with rage.

"Say goodbye, asshole Archer."

"Hold it!" shouted Frank, from the bottom of the ramp pointing his gun at Peter. "Drop it, son."

Swiveling his head, Peter looked at Frank who inched forward up the ramp. Slowly shaking his head, Peter started to laugh.

"Drop it now, or I'll fucking blow you away," commanded Frank.

Peter, with the tire iron still poised above Steven, turned away from Frank and looked down at Steven. As a horrific yell escaped his mouth, Peter thrust the tire iron at Steven's chest.

Chapter Thirty-Eight

Sunday, November 9 -- 9:13 P.M.

The sound of the gunshot deafened Steven.

Realizing Frank had fired at Peter, Steven bucked as hard as he could while twisting his shoulders to the side. Peter lurched forward, causing the sharp point of the tire iron to slam into the concrete ramp, inches from Steven's head. The force of the bullet tearing into Peter spun him sideways and knocked him backward. Peter clutched his shoulder as a large bloodstain blossomed on his shirt.

Ears still ringing, Steven could vaguely hear Peter's screams. Untangling himself from the student's legs, Steven jumped up and ran to Bobbi. Within seconds, the area swarmed with police. Steven carefully removed the gag from Bobbi's mouth while Frank and another officer cut the wire ties from her wrists.

"Thank you," she said, collapsing into Steven's arms.

Epilogue

Monday, November 10 -- 8:36 P.M.

"Ms. Cline is in room 212, just around the corner," the nurse said, pointing down the hall.

"Thanks," Steven replied. Tapping Frank on the shoulder with a cellophane-wrapped bouquet of flowers, they headed down the hall toward Bobbi's hospital room.

"Don't forget, visiting hours are over at nine o'clock," the nurse called as they rounded the corner, looking for room 212.

They found Bobbi's room, and Steven rapped lightly on the door and then they entered.

Bobbi sat in her bed reading a magazine. When she saw Steven and Frank, a huge grin spread across her face.

"Hi guys. Come on in."

Steven walked to the edge of Bobbi's bed and handed her the flowers. "These are for you. You look great."

The last time they had seen her, the paramedics were in the process of loading her into the back of an ambulance in the campus-parking garage. Her face had been ashen and she had fallen into shock, fading in and out of consciousness. Now, the color had returned to her cheeks, and her eyes appeared bright and inquisitive.

"Yeah, the nurse says you're gonna live," Frank said.

"Thanks to the two of you," Bobbi said. "If you guys hadn't shown up. Anyway, what happened to Peter? Is he dead?"

"Nah, I shot him in the shoulder. He's going to be fine. We've charged him with two counts of first-degree murder and one count of attempted murder. He confessed to the whole thing." Frank shook his head in disgust. "The punk is on suicide watch."

"So Peter must have hacked the LBS system. How did he do it?"

"First thing he did was hack the LBS system at USA Wireless to intercept the 911 calls from the victims and substitute their real location with the bogus location on the other side of town," Steven answered.

"But why did he go to all that trouble when the victims were killed in remote locations anyway?" she asked.

"He needed a way to point a finger at Jonathan. Remember, his motive for all this was to remove Jonathan from the picture, frame him for the murders and put him in prison. So he had to get the authorities to suspect Jonathan was the killer," Steven answered.

"But if Peter did the hacking, how does that frame Jonathan?" she asked.

"Peter did do the hacking, but he left Jonathan's fingerprints all over the place instead of his own," Steven answered.

"What do you mean?" she asked.

"Peter used his hacking skills to get Jonathan's user name and password. Then he masqueraded as Jonathan when he altered the LBS system so that it looked like Jonathan was doing the hacking," Steven answered.

"So when it looked like Jonathan was accessing the LBS computer, it was really Peter using Jonathan's account," Frank explained.

"I see." Bobbi nodded her head. "That makes sense. Another question, Peter chose the victims to set up Jonathan as the killer, right?"

"That's true, especially with Christina. The motive was certainly evident with her," answered Frank.

"What about Amanda, though? The motive is not as clear. If Peter had wanted to set up Jonathan, he should have stopped with Christina," Bobbi said.

"I came to the same conclusion," Frank said. "At first I thought maybe Jonathan had lost his head, raped Amanda and then killed her to shut her up. Then, when it turned out she wasn't raped, I had the same issue with lack of motive."

"So why did Peter kill her?" she asked.

"It was bugging me so I asked him. It's really the same reason he tried to get you. Peter told me that all his life others around him have had the power. Most times, in his opinion, they get the power for the wrong reasons, good looks, popularity or they're good at playing a sport."

Frank shook his head. "That sick fuck, pardon the language, told me when he strangled Christina, he finally felt the power that he deserved—the power to take a life. He said that feeling was the most intoxicating thing he had ever experienced, and he enjoyed it."

"So that's why he targeted Amanda?"

"Yes," Frank answered. "Apparently he met Amanda at the presentation in the auditorium on Saturday

351

morning. He said he was having a great conversation with her, and Jonathan stole her away. He also claimed later that afternoon Jonathan brought Amanda to the office to rub his face in it. He said he needed to teach Jonathan a lesson. I think after killing Christina, his sick mind began deteriorating quickly. I think he wanted to kill again and the situation kind of fit into his scheme to frame Jonathan."

"So that's why he targeted me," Bobbi said, nodding. "After he tied me up I remember him saying something about I should have gone out with him, and that I should have gotten to know him. He said that I would have learned to like him. When I rejected his advances, I guess he decided to teach me a lesson."

"We'll probably never know exactly what was going on in that sick brain of his," Frank replied. "The bottom line is, he had been rejected all his life, and he got fed up and decided to fight back. Unfortunately, he chose a horrible way to fight back by killing. The bastard found that he enjoyed killing. Standard psychopath."

All three of them nodded, knowing Frank had meant the *standard psychopath* comment as a joke.

"So what about the threatening email from Patricia to Jonathan?" Bobbi asked.

"Peter hacked the system to get Patricia's user name and password," Steven answered. "Peter logged in and sent the email as Patricia. Speaking of Patricia, she resigned yesterday. She said she and Larry Hershman were going to move to L.A. and start an internet porn site."

Bobbi and Frank burst into laughter.

"I'm not kidding."

"What about Jonathan?" Bobbi asked, turning serious.

"He's a free man," Steven answered, smiling. "The whole thing has traumatized him. I told him to take some time off. As much time as he needs. He feels responsible for Christina and Amanda. He's going to stay down at my beach house for a while and sort things out. He'll get through this. He's a good man."

"And you, Professor Archer? Are you going to be okay?"

Steven hesitated before answering Bobbi's question. Despite catching the killer, Dr. Herbert still planned to proceed with a disciplinary hearing against Steven. When word got around to Steven's fellow faculty members about the hearing, they had all pledged their support. There had even been talk of a strike to force the administration to drop it. Steven was grateful for the support, but he knew he was in for a long, bloody battle with the new dean.

Like Jonathan and others on his team, Steven was racked with guilt because the WILCO Project, his brainchild, had been involved in the horrible deaths of two innocent women. A lump formed in his throat. He knew it would take a long time, maybe years, for the pain caused by events of the past weekend to soften and fade away.

He managed a smile for Bobbi and answered, "I'll be just fine."

The End

Made in the USA
Charleston, SC
17 November 2010